Arches Legend

C. R. Fulton

THE CAMPGROUND KIDS
www.bakkenbooks.com

Arches Legend by C. R. Fulton
First Edition

Cover Credit: Anderson Design Group, Inc.

Disclaimer: Some of the characters in this book, though historical figures, find fresh adventures here that are purely works of fiction. Any involvement of Butch Cassidy and Colonel Percy Fawcett with Arches National Park is also fictional.

ISBN 978-1-955657-67-9
For Worldwide Distribution
Printed in the U.S.A.

Published by Bakken Books
2023

To my husband:
You are my best friend
and my very best sounding board for ideas,
plots, and stories. I'm looking forward
to the next 80 years with you.

National Park Adventures: Series One

Grand Teton Stampede

Smoky Mountain Survival

Zion Gold Rush

Rocky Mountain Challenge

Grand Canyon Rescue

National Park Adventures: Series Two

Yellowstone Sabotage

Yosemite Fortune

Acadia Discovery

Glacier Vanishing

Arches Legend

-1-

Camping gear. Considering all the times it's saved my life, I do my best to take care of it. I run my fingers over the claw marks on the front of my backpack, smiling at the memory of Cranky Bear protecting her cubs at the Smokies. But I've never camped in the desert before, so Arches National Park will be a new experience. My bed is covered in rope, fire starters, survival blankets and a book on desert camp craft.

My 14-year-old cousin Ethan sticks his head into my room. "Does that dog always bark so much?"

I look out my bedroom window at the border

collie circling wildly next door. The dog barks repeatedly, and the sound grates on my nerves. "Yep. Max loves to yip and bark."

"Mom!" my ten-year-old sister Sadie yells from her room. "Can I bring my metal detector?"

"No, sweetheart, it's too big to fit on the plane!" Mom's voice floats up from the kitchen. I hear her phone ring as I carefully stash items in my bag. A moment later, she takes Ethan's place in the doorway.

"It's for you."

I scowl when I answer the phone. "Hello?" A gravelly voice makes me stand up a little straighter. "Uncle Elliot!" We hardly ever hear from our great-uncle since we met him at Yosemite.

"Do you *still* have the compass?" The insistence I hear in his voice makes me grip the phone tighter.

"Of course I do." I pull the instrument from my pocket.

"I told you it was special but recent… Well, certain events have made it *invaluable*." I turn over the heavy brass compass in my hand. The way he says that word *invaluable* makes me wince. For an eccentric treasure hunter like him, saying that something I have is valuable beyond estimation is almost overwhelming.

"In a place like Arches, it might reveal…" He sighs, then adds, "more than I'm willing to say over the phone."

The compass is shaped like a hockey puck with a thick glass top. I press the invisible button on its side and grin as it slides open into three layers.

"I've sent you a package that should arrive within three minutes," Uncle Elliot continues. "I've been tracking the shipment closely as it contains some very important information. You kids impressed me at Yosemite with your perceptive skills. Consider this a test of sorts that I hope you pass." The phone goes silent.

I look at it, wondering, *what on earth could he mean?* Outside, Max's barking reaches a new pitch. Pulling back the curtain, I see an unfamiliar white vehicle stop in front of our house. Dropping the phone, I sprint for the stairs.

"Where's the fire?" Ethan jokes as I zoom past.

"Elliot!" is the only word I say as I leap the last few stairs. I skid through the front door, nearly ripping off the screen door with my wide shoulders.

A tall man stepping out of the car is holding a large envelope and a clipboard. He holds up a photo as I approach, checking my face against it. "Isaiah Rawlings? Please sign here."

I take the clipboard, eyeing the envelope still in his hand. I see that one end of it bulges, and I can't wait to see what's inside. I scribble my signature on the line.

"Okay, Express Delivery promises every sender a photo verification upon delivery, so if you don't mind. . . ."

He holds up his phone, and I take the package as Ethan and Sadie arrive behind me. I think of smiling too late. Then Sadie snatches the envelope out of my hand.

"HEY!" I protest, but a flash of fur makes me spin. *It wasn't Sadie!*

"Max, NO!" Sadie shouts as the dog jets down the road, the brown envelope dangling.

"After him!" I yell, watching him turn left.

Ethan and Sadie are faster runners than I am, but I put my brain to good use, cutting through the Smiths' backyard, dodging kids' toys.

Max zips past on the sidewalk, and I nearly catch him! His silky fur slips through my fingers as he whips around, eyes bright, ready to play.

"Oh, you think this is a game, huh?" I bite my lip. *I must get that package!* Sadie and Ethan arrive, breathless.

"I'll go left," Ethan whispers, easing across the quiet neighborhood street. Sadie takes a small step forward, but Max immediately jets to one side. Ethan leaps for the dog, who rushes my way, still eyeing Ethan. I leap, stretching long…my fingers close on the envelope! Skidding near the street, I growl, yanking with all my might. The package tears, but Max only makes off with a small strip of cardboard!

The hum of an engine makes me roll as a black SUV cruises slowly past. I can barely make out a passenger watching me through the dark tint of the window. A shiver of dread rushes across my chest as I tuck the package under my arm. Black glasses are perched on the man's huge nose. I watch the car until it disappears down the road, noting that its plate is from Missouri, not Kentucky.

Panting hard, I look at the now somewhat soggy package.

"Why…" Sadie is holding her side, "is that package so important?"

The thrill of another adventure makes me shiver. "Uncle Elliot said it's a test of sorts."

"What happens if we pass?"

I grin. "I have no idea."

-2-

Back in my room, I clear a space on my desk, then hesitate. "Uncle Elliot hinted at things he couldn't say over the phone." I look suspiciously at the window, and Sadie rushes to shut the curtain.

I turn over the envelope and empty it onto the desk. A book called *Bandit Invincible: The Story of Butch Cassidy* lands amid a pile of old newspaper clippings, copies of letters, and a few pictures.

"What, exactly, are we supposed to figure out?" Sadie asks, her nose crinkling on one side.

"I wish I knew." My stomach clenches. *It's entirely possible we'll fail Uncle Elliot's test.*

Ethan picks up the book. "Cassidy was a famous

thief in the Old West. Historians say he stole over $10 million during his lifetime in the 1900s."

I'm glad Ethan is familiar with the story. The photo, featuring an odd shape like a backward E, a white box, then another E, grabs my attention. Behind it, I see a black-and-white photo of a serious man with a square jaw and serious eyes.

"Look! Here's a note from Uncle Elliot!" Sadie picks it up and starts to read. "Isaiah, Sadie, and Ethan..."

"Why does he always mention me last?" Ethan interrupts.

"Somebody had to be last. Go on, Sadie," I add.

"I've been on the trail of a certain artifact my entire life. I'm not the only one interested in this item, and years of careful searching have now led me to believe Arches National Park is its final resting place. You are now in possession of all my research. Guard it well. Take special note of the articles from July 1906 and 1923. The letter from Percy Fawcett is of *utmost* importance. Put the clues together, as I dare not say more lest this package should fall into the wrong hands. Remember, *great things come in small packages that last for centuries*."

I sift through the various clippings, finding one from 1906.

THE WYOMING TIMES

3 July 1906 Cheyenne, Wyoming Page 1

NOTICE!

The Pinkerton Detective Agency has released the following information to the public: the infamous criminal, Butch Cassidy, also known as LeRoy Parker, Jim Lowe, George Cassidy, and Santiago Maxwell is no longer in North America. He and his notorious partner, the Sundance Kid, have fled to South America. The West can breathe easy again without his terrorizing presence.

"Yeah, weren't he and the Sundance Kid killed in a shoot-out in Bolivia?" Ethan asks as he lifts another article and reads the contents to us.

 The British Gazette 

Published by His Majesty's Stationery Office.

No. 9 | 9 September 1923 | 05¢

Seventh Amazon Exploration in Search of "Z"

Colonel Percy Fawcett begins his seventh Amazon exploration in search of what he calls the lost city of Z. Colonel Fawcett and a team of explorers are pursuing a legend based deep in the Amazon jungle. When questioned about the possibility of encountering hostile native tribes, he replied, "Not only is it a possibility, but a surety. One only needs to know how to deal effectively with them."

"And this must be the letter from Col. Fawcett!" Sadie gingerly flattens out an ancient sheet of paper. "It looks like it's original." We all lean in to read together.

F

Commanding Officer

10 December 1908

My dearest Nina,

I pray you and the children are well. This expedition has proven the most difficult yet. Not only have we faced unseasonable rains, treacherous landscapes, and a sickness that plagues the crew, I have lost my most valuable possession. The Navigem could have led me straight to the lost city. Three nights ago, near the junction of the Amazon River and a tributary called Madeira, we were taken at spearpoint by natives. None of the usual peacemaking gestures were effective.

We were coming from a set of ruins previously unknown to explorers, where I had found the Navigem. Carved from a Ceylon sapphire, the gem fit perfectly in the palm of my hand. On its beautiful blue surface were etched symbols, which I believe are the map to the lost city.

The natives must have known that I had taken it. Another war party returned with two American prisoners. We were tied together at the wrists. The American called himself Santiago Maxwell, though I do not know the second man's name. Before the natives could torture us, I admitted to him of having found the Navigem. Maxwell convinced me he had an accomplice waiting for the right moment to break him and his partner free. My utmost concern was for the Navigem. In desperation, I handed it to him, and he assured me he would return it to a peaceful village upstream two days from thence. Gunfire suddenly echoed through the jungles, and Maxwell and his partner escaped.

I barely made it out alive; however, most of my crew did not. I found the village and waited for Maxwell to appear. I waited one full week before it became painfully obvious that I had been duped. My darling, I must find the American and the Navigem. The British crown will hear nothing of such an expedition, and I fear I must go alone. It may be a long while until you hear from me again.

My deepest love and affection,

Percy

"Hang on a minute! *Santiago Maxwell* was one of the names Cassidy used as an alibi!" Ethan says, leaning over the letter. He flips open the book. "Just as I thought…historians claim Cassidy and the Sundance Kid were killed in a shoot-out in Bolivia on November 7, 1908!"

We look at each other, "Maybe he didn't die. The real question is, where did he take the Navigem?"

-3-

As our plane lands in Utah, I look out the window; the bleak desert stretches as far as I can see. One thing is for sure, Butch Cassidy was familiar with the desert. He was born less than 200 miles from the park. After studying everything Elliot had sent, I believe it's *possible* that he had a hideout in Arches.

"Look at that!" Sadie points out my window. Towers of red sandstone puncture the flatlands.

The heat hits me like a fist as we leave the airport, the dry air is equally powerful. I can feel both draining me of energy as we settle into a rental truck for the eleven-mile trip to the park.

"If you're going to the desert, make sure you pack a *thirst aid* kit," Ethan says, emptying a pack of bright blue powder in his water. The drink turns his lips the same color, and a grin overtakes me. With Ethan, Sadie, and a national park, *anything* could happen!

We stop for our traditional picture at the welcome sign. Ethan leans against the deep brown wood.

"Ouch!" After leaping forward, he rubs his shoulder. "You could fry an egg on that sign!"

I reach out; my fingertips nearly sizzle when I touch it. Scanning the surrounding cliffs, I release a deep breath, already feeling the pressure of passing Uncle Elliot's "test."

By the time we reach the north end of the park, Ethan has told 24 more jokes.

"What kind of lion never roars?" He's completely unconcerned with the fact that none of us answer. "A *dandelion!*"

We pass a sign, and I scowl. "Devils Garden? That's what our campground is named?"

"Actually, this entire section of the park is called Devils Garden," Dad says as we turn off the highway. "And this happens to be the only campground in Arches National Park."

A heavy feeling settles over me. *What if we can't find the Navigem?* We pull into site 003, and once again, I step into the intense heat of the desert. I don't believe we've ever faced a more hostile environment or a more difficult challenge.

"So," Ethan says, studying the slick rock towers all around. "All we have to do is find one small gem hidden by a master thief over 100 years ago." He wipes the sweat from his brow. "Butch Cassidy was brilliant at what he did, and most of what he took was never found."

"Thanks, Ethan," I say, rolling my eyes.

-4-

"Let's hike the Broken Arch Trail," Mom suggests, as I finish setting a stone on each corner of my tent. It's a certainty that the solid rock under our tent won't allow me to anchor the corners with the usual tent pegs.

"So, are we going to see all 2000 arches on this trip?" Ethan asks through purple lips stained by his flavored water.

"Not if we hope to find Cassidy's hideout," I say, feeling the pressure as mere seconds tick past. *Failing Uncle Elliot's test seems a certainty.*

Sadie studies the landscape of red rocks, towers of sandstone, and sparse desert scrub set against the brilliant blue sky. "Can you imagine riding a horse through here like Butch Cassidy did? With no roads or water?" She shivers. "How did people survive back then?"

"They respected the power of the desert, and they planned for it as best they could," Dad comments as he straps on his hiking pack.

We walk down the Devils Garden Loop and come to the Broken Arch Trailhead. Slowly, I head toward the trail, feeling like I'm stepping onto an alien planet where heat and the scarcity of water rule the universe.

"If you're on a hike and find a fork in the road, what do you do?" Ethan asks.

Before we can answer his riddle, he says, "You stop for lunch!"

"We just ate lunch," Sadie says, shaking her head.

"Hey," Ethan continues, "Look at that!" He points at a tall slab of rock with an enormous boulder perched on top. "Can we go see it?"

Dad squats down, pointing at the sand. "Kids,

come look at this. See this crust on top of the sand? It's called *cyanobacteria*, and it takes hundreds of years to form. Its job is to retain moisture and create nutrients through photosynthesis. Never step off the trail into a sandy area. Even one footprint will ruin years of growth."

"So, I take that instruction as a no..." Ethan pops some candy into his mouth.

Soon, we come to a sign with arrows indicating what direction to go:

← Tapestry Arch — 300 yards

→ Broken Arch — 830 yards

"Let's go left," I say, catching a flash of motion far ahead on the trail to the Tapestry Arch.

We scramble up onto a section of solid rock. In the distance, a thin slab of stone has been hollowed out into a beautiful arch. I see a smaller arch on each side of the big one.

"Let's get closer!" Ethan's already striding in that direction.

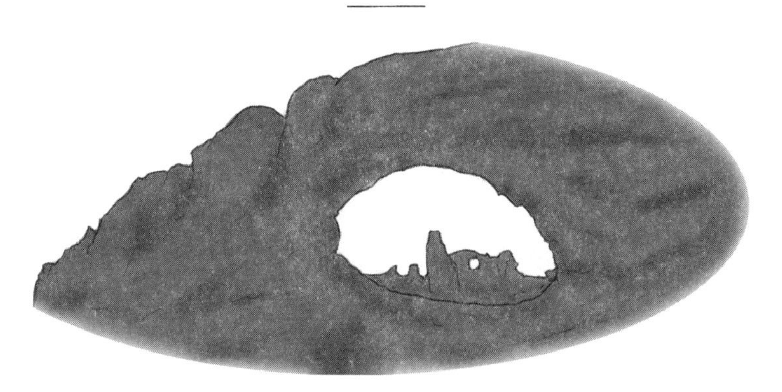

We spread out since we don't see any cyanobacteria on the solid rock, but we do notice small piles of rocks along the way. From the way they're stacked, clearly a human put them there.

"What are these for?" Sadie asks.

"Those are called *cairns*, and they mark trails through the desert," Mom answers.

Soon the massive Tapestry Arch is stretching above us.

"Wow!" I gaze up at the thousands of pounds of rock suspended above my head. *I sure hope it will stay put!*

"Hey! Listen to this!" Ethan is knocking on the wall behind the arch.

I cock my head, listening hard. “Did someone scream?”

“No, silly, listen to how hollow it sounds right here. I bet there’s a cave behind here!”

A streak of familiar energy races across my chest as I scan the valley. “No, I promise, I heard *something*.”

-5-

"Let's head to Broken Arch," Mom suggests.

"Hang on," I say, backing up against Ethan's hollow wall where the sound had seemed louder. I hold my breath, and the faint cry comes again!

"We can't leave!" I yell, rushing along the wall. Sunlight punctuates the shade as I run behind the arches. The cliffs close in, and I turn sideways to squeeze through. I step out into a valley with rock towers all around, straining to hear the cry of distress.

There! I sprint to the right, homing in on the sound.

"Help! Please help me!"

The voice is filled with urgency as I catch the sound of falling rocks in between my pounding footsteps. I veer up a slope of solid rock still running, my arms pumping.

The slab of rock I'm running on is narrow, and I dare not look down as I race across it. It ends abruptly, and my boots skid as I stop.

"Help me!" *The voice is coming from below me!* Falling to my knees, I take in the scene. The rocks had given way, and a girl dangles from the cliff's edge. *Her fingers are slipping!*

"Hold on!" I scramble down to another small ledge, desperate to reach her. A shower of pebbles rains down on her curly brown hair. Her wild green eyes fill with tears as she focuses all her strength into her fingertips. Finding room to kneel on only one knee, I reach for her. "Take my hand!"

"I can't!" she cries as she slips farther.

There's no time! Fighting the effects of the dizzying height, I stretch with a final lunge for her wrist. The instant my fingers grip her arm, she loses her hold and screams! Her weight pulls me forward, and now we're both going over the cliff!

"Got you!" Ethan cries as he snatches the back of my shirt. My forward motion comes to an abrupt halt, and I nearly lose the girl who's thrashing wildly for a better handhold.

"Stop! Hold still!" I roar. "Look at me!" With nothing but hundreds of feet of air below us, her emerald eyes finally lock on mine. "Okay, I've got you! But you must hold still!"

With a whimper, she obeys, casting a gaze downward.

"Just look at me," I encourage, listening to the fibers of my shirt ripping under both our weights. "Ethan, we need a solution, NOW!"

"I am..." He groans, unable to pull us both up.

A spray of pebbles pelts my neck. The girl cringes as they hit her in the face. The slick of sweat makes my grip slide against her skin. "No!"

-6-

"Okay, okay!" I hear the desperation in Sadie's voice as she takes in the perilous scene. "Hold on a minute longer, Isaiah. You can do it," she encourages me.

"I'm...trying..." I groan, my muscles straining.

I hear movement above me and then see a rope unfurl against the sky. The girl snatches at it with her free hand.

"Good job!" I grunt as the neck of my T-shirt rips. "Hurry!"

"It's tied off; I'm coming down!" Sadie eases past Ethan, towing another length of rope. In seconds, she's got it tied around my waist.

"I'm going to pull you up!" She rushes back to the top as I consider the absurdity of her statement. *It's impossible! What if the girl I'm holding can't keep hold of the rope? My grip is slipping!*

Clearly, the girl is thinking the same thing because she begins to struggle again.

"Hey, stop! I promise, I will not let go. I've got you; just lock eyes with me!" Maintaining eye contact seems to be the only thing that calms her. Ethan adjusts his grip on my shirt, and the rope cuts into my ribs. Trusting it, I let go of the cliff and take hold of the girl's wrist with both hands.

One more yank and the ropes draw us over the edge! We fall in a heap, and the girl rests her head on my shoulder. We lie there and breathe for a moment, enjoying the feel of the solid rock beneath us.

"Sadie, how on earth did you do that?" I ask.

Grinning, she poses, flexing her muscles. Then Dad steps from behind her and flexes his. I laugh, then scramble to my feet and study the girl who's still trembling from the ordeal.

"What happened?" Mom asks, rushing up with one hand over her heart.

I felt like the girl and I had dangled there for hours, but in reality, I guess only a few seconds had passed.

"I heard her cry..." I say, turning to the girl and finding bright green eyes searching my face.

She swallows hard. "I... The rocks gave way, and I started to fall!"

I turn, studying Sadie's work with the ropes. "How did you do that so fast?"

"I guess adrenaline and sugar have the same effect on me!" Sadie grins.

Mom steps to the edge to look over. "You almost fell from here?!"

"I was... Well, my name is Mahloan." She turns toward me. "Thank you for saving me."

"Sure thing," I say.

Once we've all introduced ourselves, Dad asks, "Well, Mahloan, we're heading to Broken Arch. Would you like to hike along with us?"

"That might be safer!" she answers with a mischievous glint in her eyes.

"Aren't your parents here?" Mom asks.

Mahloan shakes her head. "No. I live nearby with my grandmother who is very sick. She has been asking for a plant named bathua to make her feel better, and I've been trying to find some."

For the first time, I notice a leather bag with a strap across her chest. She's just a smidge shorter than me, and I'm glad to see she has quit trembling.

"When's lunch?" Ethan asks.

"We've already discussed this," Sadie says.

"Oh, right. Bummer. At least we can't starve in the desert, though."

"Why?" Sadie asks as I coil up the rope.

"Because of all the *sand-which-is* here!"

The rope gets stuck under a boulder, Mahloan pulls it free, handing the end to me. Her voice is quiet. "Thank you again."

I think her emerald eyes might just contain all the mysteries of Arches.

-7-

Listening to our conversation as we walk the narrow trail to Broken Arch, Mahloan comments, “You all seem really interested in Butch Cassidy.”

“Well, you’re here looking for bathua, and we’re also searching for something,” I say.

Sadie’s expressive eyes widen at my answer. “Isaiah….”

The way she looks makes me shrug. “What? She might be able to help us.”

Sadie frowns, shaking her head.

“I live right beside the park across the Colorado River. My family has owned the land for generations, but…” Mahloan shakes her head as she and

Ethan walk ahead of us. "Anyway, I've practically grown up in this place."

"See?" I whisper, nudging Sadie. "Give me one reason why we *shouldn't* trust her."

"I just…"

"So, you've got no reason," I state.

"Something doesn't sit right about her," she replies, crossing her arms.

"Like I said, *no reason*. Have you noticed we're making no progress toward the Navigem? Zero. Nada. Zilch."

"Ugh!" Sadie groans softly.

"So, Mahloan…" I say, hurrying forward. "Do you know of any evidence that Butch Cassidy spent time here before this place was turned into a national park?"

She cocks her head in thought. "Let me think about it."

We walk in silence for a bit until Ethan trips.

"Ouch! Oh! That stings; I just know it's going to leave a mark!"

He's gripping his leg where a patch of long spines has pierced the skin.

Mahloan looks at the side of the trail. "You brushed into a Whipple's fishhook cactus."

"Who would leave *fish hooks* out here?" Ethan cries.

"Just stay still, and I'll take care of it." Mahloan searches through her leather satchel, pulling out a pair of tweezers. "This isn't going to hurt…me."

I laugh at the glint in her eyes as she removes the spines. Ethan squeaks every time she yanks one out.

"That's the thing about a lot of cactuses, especially this one. The spines have tiny hooks all over them that cause them dig in deeper," Mahloan states calmly.

"I feel it… Now that you mention them, I feel those hooks!"

I turn, shaking my head at his drama. We're on a plateau, and I see a sheer tower with crumbling rocks all around its base in the distance. Something shifts among the boulders in the distance, and I study the spot, trying not to focus on anything in particular. I have found that's the best way to catch motion. The effort pays off, and I see movement again from the corner of my eye. *Whatever I'm seeing must be the same color as the stone.*

I pull out binoculars as Ethan shouts, "Ohhh! Ouch! It burns!"

I adjust the focus and gasp! A lion is staring right at me! I whip down the binoculars, stepping back. *I sure felt like he was right there in front of me!*

"What is it?" Sadie asks, staring at my ashen-colored face.

"L…lion!" I point at the distant tower, but I can't pick him out again. Sadie takes over the binoculars but can't spot him either.

"You're sure you saw a cougar?" Mahloan looks up from removing the spines.

I notice her eyes are similar in color to the cougar's. "Yeah, I've *always* wanted to see one!"

"I'm confused. Is it a lion or a cougar?" asked Ethan.

Sadie, the walking animal encyclopedia, pipes up, "A cougar *is* a lion—a mountain lion, Ethan. They are also called by other names, including *puma, panther*, and *catamount*."

Mahloan twists, scanning the rocks. "Lions—whatever their name—I *hate* lions."

"Sounds like there's a story behind that statement," I say.

"Gran and I have always raised sheep for a living. Building up a flock is difficult in the desert, but this year we lost half of them. Finally, we set up a camera and, sure enough, a cougar was killing them." She yanks a spine from Ethan particularly hard at the memory.

"Ouch!"

"Sorry. Those sheep were all we had." I see Mahloan's jaw tighten at the memory; and deep inside, I wish I could help her. She pulls a thick leaf from her leather satchel. She squeezes out its juice and rubs it over Ethan's leg.

"So, lions and me...definitely not friends."

Ethan sighs in relief. "Whatever that stuff is, it feels heavenly."

"It's aloe vera." Her head comes up, one brow lowered. "Didn't Butch Cassidy have some other names?"

"George Cassidy," Sadie offers, and I'm glad she finally seems to be over her distrust.

"And Santiago Maxwell," I add.

Mahloan snaps her fingers. "That's it! I know of a place you'll want to see!"

-8-

It's late in the day when we finally pull into the visitor center. Mahloan confidently leads us inside. We walk under a model arch and end up in a section with black-and-white photos of the park.

"Let me see..." She studies the pictures and then points to one. "Right here, see these petroglyphs?"

I study the ancient writing in the pictures, wondering how they will help us. "Yeah."

"Well, right behind this area, I have seen another rock with a name carved on it..." She arches her delicate eyebrow at me, waiting for an answer.

I swallow, wishing my mouth wasn't so dry as I struggle to say the words. "Santiago Maxwell?"

"Exactly!" She grins, and the entire museum seems to light up. "I just couldn't remember exactly where it was." She points to the wall of photos. "But I know it's near Delicate Arch."

Resisting the urge to keep watching her, I turn, taking in the old photos. I squint at one picture of a cow and a calf looking at the camera with an arch in the distance.

"Hey, guys! Look at this!"

"What's so important about it?" Sadie asks, folding her arms.

"Don't you see it? That cow is wearing a brand!"

Ethan gasps and exclaims, "Cassidy's brand!"

"And that's Delicate Arch behind them!" Mahloan points out. "This picture was taken right near the Santiago signature."

"Mom, can we hike to Delicate Arch tonight?" I ask excitedly.

"It's nearly dark," she says. She and Dad walk up, holding hands. "How about we go first thing tomorrow?"

I glance at Mahloan. "Do you… Well, would you like to come with us?"

Sadie rolls her eyes as Mahloan nods.

"Yes, I'd like to scout that area for bathua."

"Taking a plant from a national park would be illegal," Sadie flatly declares.

Never mind about her not being suspicious anymore.

"Oh, I wouldn't take any plants from the park. I need to figure out where it likes to grow so I can hunt for it in the open desert." She bites her lip, tears pooling. "Gran really needs it."

"Maybe we could help you find it. I mean, we'll be seeing a lot of the park," I say, trying to make up for Sadie's sharp, biting comment.

"Yeah, we can help each other," Ethan adds.

"Perfect. Can you pick me up at the entrance tomorrow?"

I look at Mom and smile when she nods.

"Yes!"

Now we really are on Cassidy's trail! I'm almost

out of the museum when another thought strikes me. "Hold up a minute!"

I hurry back through the building, finding the photo again. Below it I read this caption: "Delicate Arch, 1927." *That's after Fawcett's letter home!*

"Wow!" I'm nearly breathless, staring at the date. This photo pretty much proves that Cassidy came back to his birthplace long after his supposed death in Bolivia. *Now, where would an outlaw like Butch Cassidy hide a small blue gem?*

I sleep little because the tent is so *hot*. It's a relief in the morning to step out into the dry air. I guzzle two bottles of water and wipe the sleepy feeling from my eyes. Today I've got to stay sharp so we don't miss any clues. Soon we're on the way to the park entrance.

"What made all these weird rock formations, anyway?" Ethan asks, dumping a packet of green powder into his water.

"There's actually a thick bed of salt deep under the earth here. And as rainwater filters down through the sandstone, some of the salt disintegrates. The effects of heat and cold force the rocks to move minutely, developing recesses that increase with every storm. The fractured rock layers become fins; as softer rock breaks away, those fins become towers. Then sometimes, if the conditions are exactly right, an arch will form as wind and sand and water break down the rock in the center."

As we pull up to the park entrance, I spot Mahloan right away. I smooth my hair as she gets into the truck.

"I was reading about Butch Cassidy last night," Mahloan says as she climbs in, her hair curling over one shoulder. "Did you know he called his Wyoming hideout 'Hole-in-the-Wall'?"

"Yes, ma'am!" Ethan says, shifting over to make more room.

"Well, I couldn't help thinking about Arches. I mean, we have holes in the wall everywhere."

"And your point is?" Ethan asks.

"What if he also had one here? The main reason

for his Wyoming hideout was so his bandit partners could meet in secret after a theft."

I lean back, struck by her words. "That could be exactly what we're looking for!"

She giggles. "Good, but what exactly are you looking for?"

Sadie turns in the front seat to scowl at me. I just roll my eyes.

"We believe Butch Cassidy hid..."

Sadie interrupts by clearing her throat loudly. So, I change my next words to appease her. "An artifact in the park."

"I have never heard of anything like that around here," Mahloan says as she settles her leather bag on her lap.

"Exactly," Ethan says. "If everyone knew where it was, we wouldn't be searching for it."

"Good point. That's kind of where I am with the bathua. Grandmother remembers it growing in a certain place when she was very young, but she can't remember where."

"Okay," Dad says, turning into a small parking area. "The trail to Delicate Arch is straight ahead."

"What happens if you go left?" Ethan points to a slim trail branching off to our left.

"That's the way to Wolfe Ranch. A small cabin still remains there," Mahloan says.

"As in, a cabin that could have been a hideout at some point?" I ask.

Sadie, Ethan, and I grin at each other.

"I say we check it out," Sadie adds, heading down the path. Within a few steps, we step onto a metal bridge crossing over a gently flowing stream.

"A stream in the desert?" Ethan asks, leaning over the rail, his shadow wavering on the cloudy water.

"It's called Salt Wash…" Mahloan responds, but Sadie cuts in.

"And there's something drowning in it!"

-9-

"How do you spot stuff like that?" I ask, but Sadie is already racing off the bridge toward a weak splashing downstream.

She disappears momentarily in the tall, thick grass growing at its edge. All I see is her arm shoot out to snatch a dripping black lump from the water.

"It's a raven!" Her voice echoes from the grass. "I need help!"

We find her cradling a very bedraggled bird.

"He's tangled in a fishing line!"

Mahloan tries to get it off without success. "It's so tight that it's cutting into his legs!"

"Here, let me try." I pull out my multi-tool and

take a second to decide which tool would work best. The poor bird is breathing in ragged gasps. "Is it going to live?"

"Yes, he's just exhausted from trying to swim for so long," Mahloan answers.

"If you say so." I snap open a small blade on the tool and carefully trim the line.

"What do you call two crows who stick close together?"

I stop working and stare at Ethan.

"Velcrow!"

I roll my eyes then cut two more pieces of line.

"Here, let me see…" Sadie carefully counts the large feathers on the bird's wing. "Just as I thought, he has 17 pinion feathers, so he's definitely a raven. Crows only have 16."

"Well, that just makes it all a matter of *a-pinion!* Ha ha!" Ethan cackles at his own joke.

"Poor guy, you only have to hear these jokes for a little longer," I say. "Mahloan, please keep some tension on this, will you?"

Her eyes are like their own universe, and I struggle not to stare at her as she takes the nearly invisible line. Cutting a few more tangles, I only have one piece left to cut. It's wrapped so tight around his lower leg that his scaly skin is swollen. "You better hold him tight, Sadie. Removing this final strand won't be comfortable."

The raven makes a strange sound after I cut the last loop. "*Rawhh.*"

"You're welcome!" Sadie says happily.

"Let's go check out the cabin."

We join Mom and Dad at the slightly sagging log cabin with only one main room. Intense heat billows out the door.

"I've only got one question..." Ethan says. "Where did they get the trees or lumber to build this cabin?"

I run a hand over the ancient logs, scanning the barren landscape. Sadie squats, holding the bird in her lap, and sifts through the sand in the building's shade. She holds up shards of translucent blue rock. I look at her sharply, and she raises her brows as she shifts the pieces in her palm. The bird's eyes glimmer brightly as he watches. Sadie tucks the pieces back under the sand and stands up.

"Why on earth would anyone live here?" I question as I feel the sun beating down on me. A red flush creeps up my neck as I realize Mahloan lives only a few miles from here.

She just giggles. "The desert isn't for everyone, but it's in my blood, and that's why..." She abruptly closes her mouth tightly.

The raven wiggles in Sadie's arms. *"Caaaaw!"*

"Oh," Sadie croons, "I'm so glad you're feeling better!"

Ethan sticks his head into the cabin over the half door that's nailed there. "Whew, it's hot! Hang on...what's that?" He points.

-10-

I lean over the door, squinting into the dimness of the interior. "Where?"

Ethan points to a hand-hewn log that looks like it might have been a mantelpiece over a fireplace. I see some letters and symbols that have been etched into the wood. "S.K. Then there's…possibly an elephant's head, the shape of an eye, and then a circle," he says.

"It's not an eye; it's an arch," I say.

"It could be."

"S. K.?" Sadie leans over the door with the raven in her arms to take a look. "S.K. probably stands for Sundance Kid!"

The bird is holding up his head now, and he studies me with one inky black eye.

I nod, studying the symbols and memorizing everything. "I think we just found a clue."

"A clue to what?" Mahloan asks, squeezing in to look.

"To…" I start to say until I notice Sadie and the bird squinting at me. "Well, our uncle asked us to look for some things."

Mahloan shrugs, grinning at me. "Then I know you'll be really excited about what I'm going to show you next. Come on!"

We turn to follow her as the desert sun beats down. Sadie sets down the raven, but he flops onto his side. "Hmmm. Maybe you need a bit more supervision before I let you go."

She's perfectly happy to continue holding the raven in her arms as we cross Salt Wash.

"Everybody, drink something!" Mom calls. She doesn't have to tell me twice.

I stop to pull out a bottle and when we start

walking again, I find Sadie and I are well behind everyone else.

"Why don't you like Mahloan?" I prod.

She sighs. "It's not that I don't like her. I just don't trust something about her."

I frown. "If you're going to keep treating her that way, you'd better come up with a reason for it."

Sadie groans, shifting the raven. "I'm telling you, Isaiah, be careful what you share with her. Have you forgotten Uncle Elliot's warning?"

The raven lays his beak over her shoulder as if hugging her neck. "Oh, poor baby, you had a rough day, and look, your beak is chipped!"

I lean in to look carefully. "Looks like that happened a long time ago."

"Chip! *Chip* is the perfect name for him."

"You can't keep him, Sadie," I warn, wanting to get back at her for not trusting Mahloan.

"I know. As soon as he can fly, I'll let him go."

I cringe as a scream echoes across the desert!

-11-

I sprint over a low hill and see Mom, Dad, Ethan and Mahloan frozen in place, staring at the path.

"Don't move, Mahloan!" The tone of Dad's voice sends a chill down my spine.

At her feet lies a tightly coiled rattlesnake, its vibrating tail creating a loud buzz. Sadie skids up next to me, her face white.

"Isaiah, see that stick over there?" Dad asks without moving.

My throat is too dry to speak. I swallow hard and try again. "Yeah!"

"Slowly grab it and then come this way."

I'm surprised my hand doesn't tremble as my

fist closes around the twisted dry wood. Knowing snakes are agitated by vibration, I carefully place each step I take.

"What do we do?" I ask, gripping the stick like a club.

"I'm not sure…" Dad is standing several feet behind Mahloan, who is frozen in place. I can see her chest is heaving in panic.

"We better figure out something quick!" Ethan adds.

I wish I had a shield to put between Mahloan and the serpent. I look around me. *These low shrubs might just do the job!* I grip the base of one and pull. "Sadie, help me!"

She's beside me in a heartbeat, setting Chip down carefully.

"Pull!"

"Ouch!"

Thorns poke us as we rip the shrub from the hot sand. Chip waddles awkwardly and then flops on Sadie's feet.

Ignoring the thorns, I tear the bush in half. Armed with the stick and a section of brush, I rush toward Mahloan.

"Go slow, Isaiah!" Dad warns.

The rattler suddenly seems to condense as it coils tighter. Without warning, his wedge-shaped head, with fully extended fangs, launches toward Mahloan! Thankfully, the strike doesn't quite reach her, but his still wide-open mouth convinces me he's serious.

"Mahloan! Step backward, slowly and carefully." Dad keeps his voice low.

"I…ca…can't." Mahloan's breath is coming in tiny gasps.

What if she faints and falls toward the snake? my mind screams.

"Okay." Dad is thinking fast. "Isaiah, hand me the stick."

"But Dad, I'm closer to the snake!" I'm completely focused on the snake.

"You're right," he admits.

I inch forward without breathing. Three more silent steps and I'm right behind Mahloan. I hear her moan, and I know there's no time.

The snake coils again, and before I can rethink my plan, I jam the shrub between her and the serpent. With my other hand, I grip her shoulder and shove her backward.

She runs as the snake strikes the branches, and I leap skyward!

"Get out of there, Isaiah!" Dad's voice penetrates my focus, and I sprint away from the rattlesnake.

Mom wraps Mahloan in a tight embrace, and I begin walking in a large circle, burning off the surging adrenaline.

The snake makes a hasty exit, and Dad crouches, rubbing his eyes. "That was close."

"Caw, caw, caw," Chip says, safe in Sadie's arms.

"Why was the snake mad at the jewel thief?" Ethan quips and then answers. "Because he wanted his *diamondback!*"

I can barely produce an empty laugh.

Mahloan turns my way with tears pooling in her eyes. "I… Why…why would you do that?"

I shrug. "You needed help."

"But that snake could have bitten you."

"Well, Mahloan, that snake was *going* to bite you and even tried," I say.

"Mahloan, you can count on my brother being brave. But, then again, there's a fine line between brave and stupid."

I put my hands on my hips. "I can't tell if that was a compliment or an insult?"

Sadie merely shrugs in response.

"How about seeing those markings?" Ethan expertly changes the subject, wiping his brow. "We're going to bake to a crisp out here."

By the time we reach the petroglyphs, my heartbeat has returned to normal and my brain is still sharp.

"Come on," Mahloan says, leading the way while scanning carefully for snakes. "It's this way."

We follow her over a smooth slab of rock, enjoying the scant shade the tower provides. People are hiking down the trail toward Delicate Arch, and I glance over my shoulder. I jerk, twisting fully back toward the trail.

"Do you see another lion?" Ethan asks as he walks beside me.

I point, scanning the hikers. "Remember when we retrieved the envelope from the dog and a SUV drove by right then? I thought I saw the same guy hike by moments ago."

- 12 -

“Really?” Ethan straightens up as he searches the path. “You go on; I’ll keep watch.”

I nod as he saunters up to the tower and leans one shoulder against it, picking at his fingernails and looking bored, but I can tell he’s keeping a sharp watch on the trail.

“He’s wearing dark glasses and has an enormous nose.”

“Roger that.”

I duck back into the shade and hurry toward Mahloan, who is waiting with my family.

“There you are!” Mahloan turns sideways and slips through a tight crevice.

"I don't think..." I grunt, wedged between the cliffs. "...I'll fit."

Mahloan giggles. "Breathe out!"

I shrug, force out my air, and squeeze through. Sadie hardly needs to turn at all, and Chip carefully studies the area.

"Ugh, we don't fit," Dad says, his voice echoing. "Just keep watch for snakes!"

"No problem, Mr. Rawlings. It's right here."

Sadie and I gasp, staring open-mouthed at the name etched into the stone:

Santiago — C. P. F., 1925 — all debts paid.

"C. P. F.? Colonel Percy Fawcett! 1925? He took his last Amazon expedition in 1926!"

"Wait, does that mean Cassidy returned the rock?" I ask.

Sadie elbows me, and Chip seems to growl.

"Rock?" Mahloan asks.

"Yeah, Cassidy owed Fawcett a rock," Sadie says in a dry tone, refusing to offer more information.

"But if this is true, then Uncle Elliot is wrong, and there's nothing to find." Inside, I deflate. *Finding the Navigem would've been so incredible.*

"Well, Mahloan, thanks for showing this to us. I guess it's the answer we were looking for!"

How can Sadie sound so happy when this entire legend just fell apart?

"How did you find this place, anyway?" Sadie asks, heading back toward the tight crevice.

Alone, I squat in front of the inscription, running my fingers over it and longing to see something else. *Anything else.* I release a long breath. *Maybe we can still help Mahloan find the bathua.* Squeezing back through the cleft, I gaze over the desert. Its red rock and blue sky don't seem as bright as they had five minutes ago when I still had a mystery to unravel.

Mahloan and Sadie chatter happily as we hike back to Ethan, who is still keeping a sharp watch.

"Shhhhh!" His hiss makes us all fall silent. "He's right over there." Ethan's words make my blood run cold. "See him? He's trying to look busy, re-packing his bag."

That familiar sensation rushes across my chest as I catch sight of the tall man; his hooked nose is all too recognizable.

"You were right. He doubled back, and he's been trying to look like he has a reason to have stopped here the entire time," Ethan whispers so Hooknose cannot hear the conversation.

I glance at Mahloan. She's wringing her hands together as she stares at the man. "You think that guy is looking for your rock too?"

I shrug, the dark heavy feeling crushing in. "Yeah, but since Cassidy gave it back to Fawcett, nobody's gonna find anything."

"WHAT?" Ethan asks, dismay etched into his features.

"Yep. You heard me. This quest from Uncle Elliot has been pointless."

-13-

Even the dancing flames of our fire seem glum. I glance over at Sadie, who's been feeding Chip bits of her food. He's good and dry now, and he's getting stronger every minute.

With my chin resting on my fist, I sigh.

"I'm proud of you, Isaiah!" Sadie says.

"For what?" All my bitterness about the situation comes out in those two words.

"For finally keeping *something* from Mahloan!"

One side of my nose wrinkles, "Huh?"

Ethan plops next to me, his lips now stained electric green.

"You made Mahloan think we had given up."

She smiles as Chip hops in a circle at her feet then opens his beak for more food. "That's a neat trick!"

"Um... Sadie? We *have* given up. It's etched in stone. Cassidy gave back the Navigem, and Fawcett carried it into the Amazon jungle. Now it's lost forever." Saying it is worse than just thinking it.

"Yeah," Ethan agrees.

"Boys..." Sadie stares at us across the fire. "You seriously believe that a crook like Cassidy would ever part with a gem that could very well be a map to untold treasure?"

I shrug, eyes wide. "I *did*."

"Oh, come on. Cassidy spent his entire life stealing things. He *loved* outsmarting people. How could a lone British explorer convince him to give up such a treasure? It's not like he had an army or even a posse. Look at this place! A man like Cassidy could've disappeared in a flash."

I scowl at the fire, letting her words penetrate my gloom.

"Here's what I think: the Pinkertons were after

him. In fact, they're the ones who chased him out of the country. He goes to South America, but he can't refrain from thieving for long, and he's also wanted there.

"Then the Bolivian Army shoots two American men, and everyone says it's Cassidy and Sundance. Right then, everything falls into place for them. The Pinkerton Agency believes he's dead, so he can return home. On the way, he steals the Navigem from Fawcett, never intending to return it."

Sadie continues, "When Fawcett shows up in Utah asking after Santiago Maxwell, he could have lost it all. So, he let Fawcett find him and gave him a fake, probably with wrong inscriptions on it to send him in the wrong direction!"

My mouth hangs open, seeing Cassidy years ago in my mind's eye, as she speaks. "Remember the blue slivers? I believe they're proof of my theory. So I'm proud of you for *finally* not trusting Mahloan."

Chip spreads his wings, shaking out all his

feathers, hopping comically in front of Sadie. "Oh, sorry, buddy," she says, handing him more to eat.

A scraping noise behind me makes my hair stand on end. "Shh!" I hiss. I twist, searching the darkness.

"Why did I say all that?" Sadie squeaks, her hands pressed to her cheeks.

"*Maybe* someone was listening. To be honest, I figured we were done, so I guess I owe you a big thank you," Isaiah says.

Dad steps out of the tent, Chip squawks, and in a flash, he's soaring away.

"Oh!" Sadie clutches her hands, both happy and sad. "Goodbye, Chip! Be careful and stay away from fishing line!"

Mom steps out, wrapping one arm around Sadie's shoulders. "You did a wonderful job of helping Chip. Now he's ready to be a wild bird again. That's what's best for him."

"I know," she says softly, still searching the dark sky for any sign of the raven.

"So where are we exploring tomorrow? Any ideas?" Dad asks, settling by the fire.

I'm still reeling from the probability that Sadie is right.

"How can we find an arch that's shaped like an eye and another that's a perfect circle?" Ethan asks, bringing up the clue from Wolfe Ranch.

"Well, we've seen seven or eight arches, so that only leaves 1,990 or so," Sadie says with a grin.

"I'd like to take the Parade of Elephants Trail," Mom says. "The first rock formation is supposed to look like elephants."

My head snaps up. "What?"

"The Parade of Elephants Trail leads to the Windows section of the park," Mom adds.

Ethan grins, and I see his teeth are now green. "That sounds perfect, Aunt Ruth."

-14-

"Nothing in this desert could qualify as the Garden of Eden," Ethan says as we drive past a sign announcing "Garden of Eden Viewpoint" on our way to the Windows. I try not to laugh, as his mouth is now the same neon pink color as the drink in his hand. He guzzles the rest as Dad parks the truck.

Mom makes us all drink an extra bottle of water as we get ready for the hike. We hear a distinctively "ravenish" voice from above. The bird wheels in a tight circle before landing at Sadie's feet.

"Chip must be feeling pretty good to have followed our car for 15 miles!" Mom grins as Sadie strokes his glossy feathers.

"Hiking with Chip sounds like the best thing ever!" Sadie says as we strap on our packs and start off. Chip hops next to her for a while and then flies ahead. He makes yet another new noise; it sure seems as if he's calling her forward.

We already have a splendid view of a massive formation of sandstone to the west. I don't see any arches, but plenty seem to be forming right here in front of us.

"Hey!" Dad says, pointing. "This is the Parade of Elephants! See them?"

Ethan frowns as he looks where Dad is pointing. "Nope."

"Look in the center of those towers. What looks like the trunk of an elephant is hanging down."

"Oh, yeah!" I exclaim as my hope of finding the Navigem springs anew.

"I still don't see it." Ethan stands with his hands on his hips.

"And the closer pinnacle looks like one that's flapping its ears!" Sadie's excited tone makes Chip do a little dance, producing noises I didn't think a bird could produce.

"Which one are you looking at?" Ethan asks as Chip flaps up to perch on top of the elephant's head.

"That one! What a wonderful bird you are!" Sadie cries.

"Here's a riddle. What's as big as an elephant but weighs nothing?"

Chip dives off the pinnacle and soars away. "Oh Ethan! Chip doesn't like your jokes. You made him fly away!"

"I didn't even get to the punchline. It's *his shadow*. Get it?"

"I get that Chip *and* his shadow are gone," Sadie grumps.

I step in between them. "Take it easy! We're after the code from Wolfe Ranch anyway, remember?"

Around the next bend, I look up to see Double Arch. The brilliant sky shows through the entwined arches.

"Does the trail end here?" I ask when the paved path runs out.

Dad pulls out his phone. "The website *myhike.com* says a smaller trail leads behind Double Arch and takes you to a cove of caves."

"Let's go!" My blood is pumping now as I scan the horizon for anything shaped like an eye. A rustle of feathers and a blast of air make me duck. Chip swoops in and lands at Sadie's feet.

"What have you got, boy?" Sadie squats, focused on Chip's beak. With a pleased sound, Chip carefully places a sliver of blue rock before her.

"Where did you find this?"

I rush up to inspect the piece, but shy away when Chip caws sharply at me.

"He definitely seems to like you the best," I mutter. "That looks like the pieces we found at Wolfe Ranch!"

"Do you think he could have flown over there that fast?"

"We've got to be at least three miles from there.

No, I don't think he could have made a six-mile round trip in that amount of time," Dad says, enjoying the bird's antics on the lonely trail.

"That means..." I repress a shiver of glee. "He found it near here."

Chip has the top of his head on the ground with one foot in the air as he looks at us upside down. "You are a good bird!" I say.

The trail to Cove of Caves isn't well marked, and eventually we end up using Dad's GPS to follow it, being careful to stay off the cyanobacteria. We're approaching another fin of rock when Dad says, "Okay, this is the end of the trail."

I groan. "There aren't even any arches!"

"Chip, where did you find that gem?" Sadie asks, and the raven takes off toward the fin. We rush forward, desperate not to miss any clues.

"Hurry!" Ethan cries. "I think I see an arch!"

-15-

From this angle, one singular arch pointing north is shaped exactly like an eye! The arch is pretty high in the fin, but in every way, the shape is the same as the code.

Ethan turns slowly, searching our surroundings for a circle of any sort. "All I see is a…Mahloan?"

My heart feels like it skips a beat. "Where?"

Ethan takes a swig of bright-blue water, pointing. "Down there."

Mahloan is examining the plants growing at the base of the fin.

Sadie crosses her arms. "In a park this size, what are the chances of running into her again?"

"Pretty high, apparently."

Mahloan looks up and waves when she spots us. I wave back as she starts our way.

"Seriously? Something fishy is going on here." Chip bounces at her feet, cawing excitedly.

"What do you call a fish who won't be quiet? *A bigmouth bass!*" Ethan jokes.

"I think you hit it on the head. Mahloan might have a big mouth as well. Why else would she want to know what we're looking for?"

"Wouldn't you want to know if you were in her place? Hush now, she's nearly here," I say.

"Any luck on finding the bathua?" Ethan calls.

She sighs, her emerald eyes lacking their normal sparkle. "Nothing. Hey, that arch looks exactly like the inscription at Wolfe Ranch!"

Sadie frowns, pinning me with a biting look.

"It sure does," I respond, glad for Mahloan's company, no matter what Sadie says. "Now we need to find the circle."

She smiles. "Maybe it's through the arch!"

"That's a great idea! Come on!"

We climb the slope of boulders; Chip definitely has it easy, flapping from one rock to the next.

Breathless, the four of us reach the bottom of the opening and ease our heads over its rim.

"Wow!" Sadie whispers. We might see for 40 miles across the desert!

"Double wow!" Mahloan points straight ahead. "There's a cave opening."

"Yes!" My shout echoes in the arch as I gaze at the circular opening. "Isn't it incredible that the Sundance Kid was right here, following Cassidy's instructions?"

Chip soars through the arch, landing at the mouth of the cave. He struts around, pecks the ground, and then flies back to us.

"Oh, thank you!" Sadie says, taking the sliver of blue from his beak.

"Is that glass?" Mahloan asks.

Sadie fingers it. Its edges have been worn by years of exposure, "I suppose it could be."

I nod. Blue glass would have been the easiest material from which Cassidy could have made a counterfeit Navigem.

"Let's go. We've got a cave to explore."

-16-

Cool air flows past us from the dark mouth of the cave. "How many lights do we have?" Mom asks, and I remember the shock of fear at Glacier when all our lights had died.

"Five," I say as we all hold out our flashlights. "Should be enough for about five hours each."

I click the first one on and shine it into the cave. I bite my lip, fearing it will only prove to be a slight cutout in the rock.

"Let's be extra careful about snakes," Dad says, and I see Mahloan cringe at his warning.

I sweep the light carefully over the floor, finding nothing—not even a back wall to the cave! Holding my breath, I step into the cool environment with a shiver. *The Navigem could be just ahead!*

Dad's right next to me, hunched under the low ceiling. "Looks like there are two tunnels. Everybody, let's stick together!"

Everyone responds, except Ethan.

"Ethan?" Dad calls.

"Coming, Uncle Greg!" He's dusting off his hands as he enters the cave.

Chip's silhouette at the entrance makes Sadie call, "I'll be back in a little while, buddy!"

Taking the left-hand tunnel because it's larger, we walk through the smooth red rock.

"I bet water carved out this tunnel," I say, admiring the winding structure. The walls are streaked with stripes of red and black.

"These colors are called *desert varnish*," Mahloan says, "which is caused by bacteria's extracting minerals from the air and binding them to the rock. Most petroglyphs are etched on desert varnish."

My breathing sounds ultra loud in the silence of

the cave as I notice some of the bright marks higher on the wall.

"You're right," I breathe, my light revealing a long section of pictures of antelopes and men.

Seeing the ancient markings makes me tread softly, as if I'm intruding into history. More tunnels branch off from the main one. I suck in a harsh breath as I shine my light into one. Its shaft drops straight down!

I step back, sweat beading on my forehead even in the cool air. "Everybody, stay to the left."

"L is for left—stay away from the left tunnel," Ethan adds, peering into the deep hole.

As we push farther into the cave, another tunnel branches toward the right. A few paces later, another one opens.

"Hang on…I think this tunnel is one big loop," Ethan says. "I'll be right back."

"Ethan!" Mom calls, but by then he's stepped out behind us.

"It is a loop!"

I glance over my shoulder and freeze. *Possibly my eyes are playing tricks on me or our lights are simply bouncing off the walls, but it surely looked like another flashlight was behind us.*

"You see him too?" Ethan whispers.

"Someone's behind us!" A million scenarios rush through my mind as I imagine Hooknose trapping us all here.

"Better keep moving," Ethan says, tugging me toward my family.

We pass over a sandy section of floor, leaving our footprints. Leading the group, Sadie gasps, making Ethan and me hurry forward. In a bend lies a pile of dust-covered artifacts.

"Is it here?" I whisper, striding forward.

Carefully I inspect the items. A rusty cast-iron pan sits partially on top of a strange metal bar with one end that's wider. A section of red flannel material is folded nearby.

Ethan pounds a fist against his leg. "No Navigem! And that pan is making me hungry!"

"Wait!" Mahloan kneels next to me, pointing to the metal tool. "This is a cattle branding iron. See the Double E's! Isn't Butch Cassidy's brand the Reverse-E, Box E?"

"You're right! But even his brand won't do for our search."

"What *is* a Navigem anyway?"

Sadie moans, knowing Ethan had blown secrecy out of the water.

"It's something Cassidy stole that we aim to get back," Sadie says.

"Well, let me remind you," Mahloan replies. "You can't take plants *or* gems from national parks."

I can't blame Mahloan, but she's made a point I hadn't really considered. It's true: whatever we find will belong to the park.

"Well, at least you could copy the map before we turn it over to the park," Ethan adds.

"There's a map on it?"

Sadie throws her hands into the air.

Frustrated, I assert, "Listen, we're all going to trust each other here!"

Another flash of light from far behind makes us all go still.

"We are not alone," Sadie whispers.

I hear a rustle behind me and turn to see Ethan has the fabric unwrapped in his hand.

"Don't eat that!" Mom whispers the command, but it's too late. Ethan's already licking ancient crumbs from the fabric.

"Ah fink it wash cornbread," he says, his eyes wide and his tongue still out.

"Cornbread? It was probably 100 years old!" Sadie squeaks.

"Eww," Mahloan echoes my thoughts.

"I was hungry!" The whispered argument halts when another light bounces down the tunnel.

"I think we should leave," Mahloan breathes, clenching her fists.

"How? We're in a tunnel. It's not like we can avoid them," Ethan says.

Longing to pass Elliot's test makes me sift my fingers through the sandy floor, desperate for some direction.

"Look! More shards of glass. You must be right, Sadie."

"I know I'm right!"

Carefully, I set the shards back in place. I hate the feeling of fear that rises from knowing someone is lurking behind us in the tunnel. "I say we run them off."

"What?" Mahloan whispers.

"Yeah." The idea grows inside me. "I bet if we all shout and run at them, they'll take off like scared jackrabbits."

"That actually sounds like fun," Dad says.

"Greg!" Mom scolds.

"Me caveman. Me do it!" Ethan beats his thin chest after replacing the fabric.

"One... Two..." My heart pounds as I crouch, digging one toe into the sand. "Three!"

"*Reeeeeeeh!*" Our roar rips the air and reverberates off the walls. I fight the urge to plug my ears as I launch forward. The light ahead swings wildly, and I charge, determined to catch them.

But by the time I reach the mouth of the cave, there's no sign of anyone—except Chip. He flaps wildly away at my sudden entrance. He swoops around and lands on Sadie's shoulder.

"Oh, man, where did they go?" I pound my fist into my palm, searching the desert.

"No worries, fellow cave people. I planted my camera at the entrance," Ethan says, reaching down for it. "Let's see… The camera was set on motion capture, and I see a shot of Chip…and another of Chip."

We crowd around to find comical photos of the raven's investigation of the camera. The next one is of the inside of his mouth.

"He's so cute!" Sadie croons.

Ethan swipes through tons of similar photos. "Aha! Just as I thought: it's old Hooknose himself."

I study the face. In the picture he's holding his

glasses. I see a stony expression in his eyes that makes me shudder.

Mahloan turns, sifting through her leather satchel as Sadie looks suspiciously at the surrounding rocks. "I wonder where they went?"

"I bet they hid in the loop tunnel since there isn't a photo of them running back out," Mahloan says, proving her worth.

"The question is, where should we go next? This was one big dead-end."

-17-

Mom's phone chirps repeatedly in the cool of early morning. "It must have grabbed service for just a second!"

I stare at the single glowing ember in our firepit. I can identify with it. Hope for finding the Navigem is flickering out as well. I snap a dry twig into tiny bits as clues run through my mind, providing zero new information.

"Isaiah, there's a message for you." Mom hands me her phone.

My stomach does a somersault when I see the name *Elliot Elkland* above the text that reads, **Call me ASAP for a status update.**

I release a harsh breath, wishing I could crawl into a hole and hide there. Having to tell Elliot about our complete failure seems like blowing a giant hole in the boat we're sailing on.

"We'll drive down to the visitor center after breakfast so you can call him. Besides, we need to report those artifacts we found to the rangers."

"Oh."

Mom cocks her head. "What's up? I thought you would be happy to get to talk to him."

I shrug. "We're out of clues. Failure doesn't seem like a great report."

"Have you done your best?"

I search for anything I could've done differently. "Yeah, but it still wasn't good enough."

"As you grow, you'll have *plenty* of opportunities to look down on yourself. I'll tell you a secret," she whispers. "Strong, successful people face the same failures and hardships as everyone else. The difference is they *don't quit*. The night is always darkest before the dawn."

Deep inside, I know she's right, but I feel like a boulder is sitting on my chest.

Ethan stumbles out of our tent, rubbing his eyes and dragging his pack behind. He plops next to me and digs in his bag. His rummaging forces stuff over the top. I gather the things that fall, inspecting one of them.

"What's this?" I ask, fingering a small slim disc that's white and black with an apple in the center.

Ethan yawns before responding. "I kept losing things—Mom's keys, Dad's phone, the TV remote, so my parents bought these tracking devices called Air Tags. I have an app on my phone that keeps track of whatever I attach it to. Of course, I'd have to have cell service."

"Oh," I say, as he stuffs a piece of Jolly Rancher hard candy into his mouth.

All too soon, we're parking at the visitor center, and my palms are sweating as I rehearse my failure speech in my mind.

"Perfect! Two bars! Dad will stay here with you

while I head in to tell the rangers about the caves."
Mom hops out. Ethan and Sadie follow her, and I have no more reasons to delay.

He answers, and everything floods out. "We found the codes and followed them, but it only led to a brand and some ancient crumbs!"

My voice cracks on the last word, making me sound even more pitiful.

"Cassidy's brand? That's a huge find! I'll want to see it as soon as possible."

"Uncle Elliot, it's illegal to take things from a national park," I say, rebalancing now that he knows everything.

"Ah. I keep forgetting that."

"Looks like we'll never find the item anyway."

"Precisely why I requested a call, my boy! Some added information has come to light, and it should be arriving in…two and a half minutes."

Goosebumps race across my skin as I sit up straight, searching the parking lot for the white SUV.

"If…the item is so important, why don't you come down and help us?"

He chuckles. "Funny thing about that. I *was* there a few weeks ago. National parks have a lot of rules. I suppose I *might* have been breaking one or more of them as I searched." He sighs. "They told me never to come back, but according to my calculations, you've got company."

He hangs up, and the white SUV parks right beside us. I blink at his crisp knock on my window.

"Hello again," the deliveryman says, smiling.

I offer a weak wave, shocked at the precision of his timing.

"You know the drill: sign here and then smile for the picture."

We complete the transaction quickly, then Dad asks, "How much does your delivery service cost?"

"Sir, if you have a certain package in mind, I'll draw you up a quote. Individual prices, however, are *confidential*. Have an enjoyable day!"

I stare at the package in my lap. It's far thinner

than the last one. Ethan and Sadie hop back in along with Mom.

"What's that?"

I can't formulate an answer. I hold my breath as I rip open the top and pull out a sheaf of yellowed papers covered with drawings of gears, tiny screws, and hinges. The top corner of the entire stack of paper is black at the edge, and the corner is missing.

"He sent us half-burnt gibberish?" Sadie frowns.

Mouth open, I study the first sheet, struggling to read the fancy handwriting at the top.

> Brass compass, 1912
> Design and fabrication by Empress Precision Watch Company. To be completed within six months of order placed by Robert Perry; Chicago, Ohio. Finished product must be completely waterproof.

"It's a schematic!" I breathe.

"A *ski-what*?"

"It's a technical drawing like something they would use to build equipment."

"Huh." She scowls at the papers.

I hand her and Ethan pages from the thick stack. "Let's keep them in order; that could be very important."

Dad drives back toward camp while we pore over the pages. Ethan releases a sharp breath.

"What?" Sadie and I cry in unison.

"This..." He runs his finger over the aged paper, "is for the middle level of your compass—the one with all the squiggles on it." He points to a drawing of a metal plate with small cutouts in random spots. "This page says this plate is magnetic. Why?"

"Hang on." I sift through the stack. "I think these go with the middle level too."

The top of one sheet has more instructions:

> Client expressly desired the plate to be made of steel with ferromagnetic metals embedded at the ends of each slot. Empress

Precision smelted a mixture of nickel and iron for this purpose.

"None of this schematic makes any sense at all to me!" Sadie wails.

"Sure, it does. It means the center level of the compass uses magnetic energy!" Ethan says.

"*Ooohh.* How exciting..." But Sadie's monotone voice says the opposite.

I pull out the compass, admiring its polished surface and imagining the great explorer, Robert Perry, ordering it. I compress the invisible button, and it spreads open. The middle level has squiggles on it, but now I have the power of knowledge. Magnets lie beneath its white surface. If I can only figure out how and why, we might complete this mission.

-18-

"I sure wish we had all the pages!" Ethan is still poring over the schematic as Mom fries grilled cheese sandwiches at the campfire.

"Let's head out to the Double Arch and Dark Angel today," Dad says.

"What's up with all the weird names in this park?" Sadie asks. "Garden of Eden, Devils Garden, Dark Angel?"

Mom shrugs, "I don't know where the names came from, but the hike sounds great. It's a little longer, right?"

"Primitive Loop Trail is 2.2 miles one way. So, we'd better bring plenty of water," Dad responds.

I glance at Ethan, whose lips are now bright green. *At least we can tell if he's hydrated by his chameleon colors.*

By the time we've admired Double Arch, Dark Angel has appeared in the distance.

Staring at the tall tower of desert varnished rock, Sadie shivers. "It gives me the creeps!"

The 150-foot-tall rock is shaped like a finger.

"There are supposed to be really neat petroglyphs inscribed on it," Dad says.

I can't hold back a moan. The sun seems like a punishment, and I'm not sweating anymore.

"Honey, you don't look so good," Mom says.

"Mmmm." My lips are stuck together, and I'm completely out of energy. Mom takes my arm and propels me toward a patch of shade.

"How many times have you used the restroom today?"

I shrug, my thoughts like syrup. *I don't think I've needed to go at all.*

"Ethan! I need a pack of your electrolytes right

now!" Mom sounds really worried as I lean on the rock. My legs don't want to hold me up anymore, so I slide down. *She's pressing a bottle against my lips; but my stomach is too sour to drink it.* I turn my head away.

"So help me, Isaiah! I will force you to drink if I have to!" Mom's voice convinces me to take a sip.

My mouth seems to soak it up, and suddenly I'm guzzling it down, thirst overtaking me. Mom smiles when I ask for another. Ethan hands her one then wanders toward Dark Angel.

"Hey! What does bathua look like?" His voice echoes toward us. Excitement ripples down my spine, and I try to get up.

"Oh, no, you're taking a rest," Mom insists, and I grump as Ethan and Sadie study a patch of plants. Finally, they come toward us.

"I think it might be what Mahloan is looking for," Sadie says, kneeling before me. "Are you all right?"

"Yeah, I'm better now."

A distant caw makes Sadie spin. "Chip!"

The raven lands on the ground and then hops energetically toward Sadie. Today he has a strip of blue fabric in his beak. He lays it at her feet, then bounces in a tight circle, making a happy rumbling sound.

"Oh, thank you! What a wonderful bird!" Sadie ties the fabric around her ponytail, and Chip flies up to her shoulder and gives it a gentle tug.

"Maybe you should show him the bathua. If he knows you're interested in it, he might find some more," I say.

"Great idea!" Sadie and Chip head over to the patch of plants. Sadie's hilarious, loving on the plants, showing each leaf to Chip as if it's made of gold.

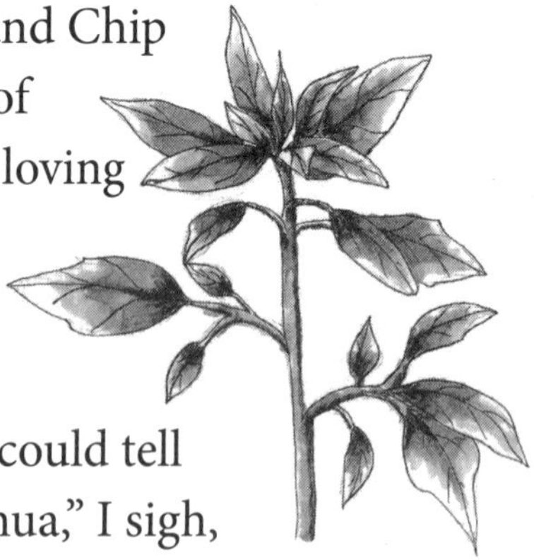

"Mom, I sure wish I could tell Mahloan about the bathua," I sigh, knowing we might never bump into her again.

"Sure, I got her Gran's phone number while she was with us. It seemed like a good idea after the rattler and the way we met her. You're a genuine hero, you know?"

I shrug. "Doesn't feel like it. I only did what I could."

"Exactly." Mom smiles. "Even heroes will need to wear a hat on the way back, however."

"What I really want is an umbrella!"

"I wish we had one. You'll need to stay out of the sun as much as possible today. That probably means in the tent."

I groan, knowing how hot that will be. Plus, the day we leave Arches is looming closer, and I still have a Navigem to find!

-19-

“Mahloan?” I whisper, wondering if I’m seeing a mirage. The 2.2 miles in the blazing sun has made the queasy feeling return.

“Hello!” she calls. “Fancy meeting you here.” Her bright grin makes me feel better. It seems like I wanted to tell her something.

“We found bathua!” Ethan proclaims.

Oh yeah, that was it.

“WHAT?!” Mahloan’s hands cover her mouth as tears glitter in her eyes.

“At least I think so.”

“Isaiah, you need to get right in the truck,” Mom urges, guiding me through the parking lot.

"Mahloan, can you come with us?" Having her company is the only way I could bear sitting out the rest of the day. "I think I've got a bit of sun poisoning."

"Oh, no," she says compassionately.

"We'll tell you all about the bathua." I might be begging, but I'm okay with that.

"Well, that sounds great!"

I smile as air conditioning washes away the heat from my skin. It doesn't take long for us to reach the campground—not even long enough for Sadie and Ethan to tell her everything about the plant.

"I can't believe it actually exists here! I was beginning to doubt Gran's memories."

"I know exactly what you mean," I mutter, sipping more water.

"Still no luck on your artifact?" she asks, her green eyes warm.

Dad parks, and I pull out the compass. "I think this might be the key."

"Wow! May I see it?"

Pleased at her amazement, I press the button and hand it to her. It opens like a flower in her hand, and she gasps. "It's beautiful!"

Maybe Sadie has finally decided to trust Mahloan because she doesn't freak out.

Mom turns. "Why don't you kids stay in here? We'll leave the air on. I think the coolness will do Isaiah some good."

We're all thankful for the cool air, and soon the four of us are examining the schematic and compass.

"Look at this." Mahloan holds up the compass. "The second level has a secret compartment!" We lean in with our heads pressed together. "See the marks where it opens?"

The compartment is barely visible because the compass is so well-constructed, but I see she's right.

"It must be like a little drawer or another level!" Sadie says excitedly.

Carefully I take it from Mahloan, searching for

a button like the main one, but I find nothing. Just like the rest of this quest, it's going to be harder than I thought.

Frustrated, I hand it back to Mahloan and begin to study the schematics again.

"What's this?" she asks. I hear a sliding sound, and we all gasp.

-20-

A slim stick of brass is protruding from the base of the compass. Slowly, even thinner arms unfold from the end of the first.

"What could it be for?" Sadie breathes.

Mahloan lofts the compass to her eye, squinting as she gazes down the shaft. "I think it's a sight—like what would be on a gun."

Ethan holds up his arms in surrender. After all, she is pointing it at his chest.

"Don't shoot!" he yells.

Mahloan grins. "Here, you try it, Isaiah."

I repeat her motion, repressing a shiver of delight. *Could this lead the way to the Navigem?* Gazing down the metal bar, I see the small arms form a distinct shape—one it seems like I should recognize. But no matter how hard I search my mind, I can't quite place it.

Soon, we've all had a turn, with no brilliant ideas. "I sure wish we had all the pages from Empress Precision."

"At this point, I'd say we have had a pretty good day," Ethan says through purple lips. "We've proved bathua grows in Utah, and we've made additional discoveries about the compass."

"And even gotten a slight case of sun poisoning," I add.

"I wasn't counting that as a plus…but I will give you one more good thing. Knock knock."

The truck is eerily silent.

"Oh, come on!"

"Who's there? But only because you found bathua," Mahloan says.

"A little old lady."

"A little old lady who?"

"I didn't know you could yodel!"

Mahloan giggles, which makes me laugh.

"You're welcome," Ethan says. "Well, I'm bored just sitting here." Ethan opens his door, and a wall of heat invades our cool environment. He immediately slams the door shut again. "On second thought, here sounds pretty good."

He takes the compass and points the sight out the windshield. "NO WAY!"

-21-

Now in the town of Moab, I dig my spoon deep into an ice cream sundae with a grin.

"Do you think we'll ever find the right rock?" Sadie asks, referring to Ethan's discovery that the compass sights form Cassidy's brand when pointed at a certain rock tower.

"Considering that the rock in question might be in any of three states where Cassidy spent time, that's a *big* maybe," Mahloan says and then bites a maraschino cherry off the stem.

"But it simply doesn't make any sense that Robert Perry would have the compass built with Cassidy's brand. The two men are opposites; and as far as we know, they never met," I say, stewing on the problem.

"Here's what I think. The sight was probably meant to do something else and happens to look like Cassidy's brand—reverse E and all. So probably whenever Cassidy got hold of it, he used that feature as a part of the trail he left."

"I bet he and the Sundance Kid were somehow separated. Maybe they didn't want the Pinkerton Agency to discover them, so they split up to be less recognizable," Sadie offers. Then she looks glumly at her plain dish of sugar-free vanilla ice cream.

"Here," I say, carefully calculating how much hot fudge I dare to give her. I plop a tiny drop on her ice cream, and she smiles at me.

"Thanks. You're the best brother."

Mahloan grows still. "I haven't ever met a family who loves each other like you all do."

I give Sadie a sly look. "Yeah, well, I'm stuck with her most of the time, so I figure we ought to get along."

She rolls her eyes, eating the hot fudge. "Yum!"

The bell above the door dings as a park ranger enters, wiping her brow.

Waving the lady ranger over, Mom asks, "Did you find the artifacts?"

"No, actually we didn't. I just returned from the Cove of Caves; and although you did indeed discover a previously unknown cave, we found no artifacts of any kind inside."

Ethan's spoon clatters to the floor. "What? Did you follow the left-hand tunnel?"

"Yes, we did. In fact, we walked well past your fresh footprints. We're incredibly pleased to have found more petroglyphs in the park, though."

"You didn't even find some red flannel fabric?"

"No, sir," she responds.

"Hmmm…it was stolen then." Ethan strokes his chin. "Whoever made that cornbread was an excellent cook."

"You ate something you found in the cave?"

"It was only a few crumbs," Ethan says, finding

a clean spoon for his massive multicolored mound of ice cream.

Sadie's wiggling in her seat, and I worry I'd given her too much sugar. I'm afraid she'll turn into a human tornado and destroy the ice cream shop. I look up to find Mahloan's face pale. She sets down her spoon and stares at nothing.

The ranger heads to the counter.

"Idea!" Sadie shouts, then slaps her hand over her mouth, eyes bulging on the edge of sugar crazy.

"Take it easy," I warn, shifting in my chair, ready to pounce if she goes wild.

"I know where to point the compass!" Apparently and thankfully, the sugar has only overtaken her volume control.

"The Santiago Maxwell signature is at a delicate arch right where he convinced Fawcett he'd given him the real thing!"

So far, she's been spot on about Cassidy. I look out at the setting sun, knowing we'll have to wait until tomorrow.

"We'll try it!" I say, and we all put our heads and hands together. "Find the Navigem and stay one step ahead of Hooknose the thief!"

Our hands fly skyward. *This plan just might work.*

-22-

The next day Mahloan spreads out a well-marked map in front of us.

"What are all the blue X's?" Ethan asks around a mouthful of Skittles.

"All the places I've searched for bathua. They are blue because they are empty, and being unable to find this plant makes me so sad."

"At least you've got one red X!" Sadie points next to Dark Angel.

"Yes! That means there could be more. See here?" She traces her finger past the Garden of Eden, the Parade of Elephants, and the Windows section. "From South Window Arch, it's only two miles to the park border, which is the Colorado River. Gran's ranch starts on the far bank and stretches for miles in every direction." She traces out a large square. "My home…" Tears prick her eyes, and I determine to find more bathua for her.

She shakes her head, clearing the tears. "But today…" She moves her finger northeast. "We're back near Wolfe Ranch and Delicate Arch."

Chip caws from Sadie's shoulder, making her plug her ear. "Yes, that's where we found you!"

The bird walks sideways down her arm until she's holding him like a baby, just as she had when he was sopping wet.

"I think he really understands English…seriously," Sadie says, nuzzling his coal-black feathers.

Ethan reaches out to touch him but Chip flaps away, blowing Sadie's ponytail to one side.

"I guess he only likes you!" Ethan says, watching the raven.

"All right, we're ready!" Mom says, adjusting her pack.

Chip lands on top of Sadie's head as she marches ahead of us. I prepare myself for the probability of this place not being the right spot. Mom's words come back to mind. *We'll keep searching and do our best.*

It doesn't take long to reach Delicate Arch, and the freestanding arch of stone with no fins or towers around makes me grin. To me, the arch really looks like a pair of cowboy chaps that froze midstride in the desert.

"How did the cowboy get so rich?" Ethan pauses, and before we can answer, he says, "His horse gave him a couple of bucks every day!"

A nearby hiker bursts out laughing, so Ethan continues. "Why did the bowlegged cowboy lose his job? He couldn't keep his calves together!"

I roll my eyes as we wait for a turn to get near the arch. People pose under it, and we wait for what seems like an eternity. I take a deep breath as we step up to it, pulling out the compass and opening the sight.

"Go on!" Sadie urges confidently.

I bite my lip and raise the sight. A loud bark of laughter escapes me! In the distance, I see a smaller square of rock. The sight makes a backward E on the left and a normal E on the right, and the rock is a perfect size for the square in the center of the brand.

"What is it?" Sadie hangs on my arm.

"It's Cassidy's brand!" I hand over the compass and memorize which rock it was. "Yes!"

Mahloan scans the area with her binoculars. "It looks like we can stay off the biological soil crust if we curve to the north."

"You mean the cyanobacteria?" Ethan asks.

"Yes…but look at that!" She points straight ahead at ancient footprints of plain sand that head straight to "our" rock. The soil crust is dark and lumpy all around the footprints, making the soft sand easy to see.

"Do you think those are actually Butch Cassidy's footprints?"

"Let's hope so!" I say. "We must be sure we don't leave any of our own."

Chip soars off of Delicate Arch above us, and Mom exclaims, "Great picture!"

-23-

I place my hand on the rock, nearly sizzling my skin. It's much taller than it had looked from far off. Chip swoops down, chirping incessantly and pushing something with his beak.

Sadie gasps. "It's the Navigem!"

She picks it up, rolling it in her palm, wide-eyed. I hurry to her side, glimpsing the strange markings on its etched blue surface.

"Uh-oh." Ethan's tone makes my hair stand on end.

I turn, goosebumps racing even in the intense heat. Hooknose is glaring at Sadie only a few feet away. My heart feels like it hits my toes. Thoughts racing, I find no way out. Mom and Dad are still up at Delicate Arch too far away to help. Besides, he'd waited until we were all behind the rock to reveal himself, so they won't even know.

"Mahloan, get the Navigem and give it to me."

Nose wrinkling, I stare at her as tears spill down her cheeks. *How does he know her name?* I clench my jaw as she steps forward *obediently*.

"I'm sorry. I'm so sorry!"

My emotions swirl at her betrayal, cutting deep.

"How could you?" My words can't be contained as she places the Navigem in Hooknose's palm.

Pain is etched on her features as she sniffs, "We were going to lose the ranch! That would kill Gran for sure, and I would be in foster care! He…he'll pay off our debt in return for my help. I…"

"Quiet, girl!" Hooknose sneers, turning to me. "Give me the compass!"

"NO!" I back against the rock, but Hooknose steps nearer to Sadie.

"Do you want your little sister to get hurt?"

I growl, knowing the compass isn't worth losing Sadie. My heart slams as I pull it out. He snatches it from my hand, and a red-hot anger boils up—at Mahloan, at failing this quest, and at myself most of all for not seeing through her.

"Go on, Mahloan. Get out of here!" Hooknose commands.

With a sob and one hand clamped over her mouth, Mahloan races away into the desert.

Hooknose glares at us coldly. "Don't you dare follow me. It wouldn't be safe."

He strides off, and I surge forward.

"Let him go, Isaiah. It's all right," Sadie says.

"All right?" I explode. "**Nothing** is all right! He has the Navigem *and* the compass!"

Sadie shrugs. "That Navigem was another fake."

I flinch. "How do you know?"

"I saw a chisel mark next to one symbol. Losing the compass is a problem though."

"No, it isn't," Ethan says easily, sipping purple water and leaning on the rock.

“Do you care to explain that?” I ask, hating myself more by the minute for being duped.

“I stuck an Air Tag on the underside of its first level. It’s tucked right near the hinge where he won’t find it for a good while. All I need is a cell signal, and we’ll know exactly where our enemy has been hiding.”

Muscles empty, I sink to the blazing hot sand, trying to absorb Mahloan’s betrayal.

“You’d better get out of the sun, Isaiah. Here, scoot in this hollow for a bit.” Sadie points to a hole in the big rock. I suppose someday it will be a new arch if it keeps eroding.

Ethan and Sadie scoot in next to me until we’re like sardines in a can, staring at the endless horizon and the heat waves rippling off the desert.

Ethan leans his head back with a sigh. Then his long finger points to the roof of our little dugout cave, and he starts laughing.

-24-

"T…th…th…" is all that will come out of my mouth as I stare at the marks etched into the stone roof. *It's an image of my compass!*

"Oh!" Sadie points from left to right as if reading. The first etching is of my compass, the next is a strange shape, almost like an upside-down raindrop, then comes an oval with marks on top of it.

"The compass will lead to the Navigem!" Ethan says in awe.

"But what's the middle step?" My voice cracks, echoing how I feel inside. Even though I'm thinking about the code, my heart burns at Mahloan.

Moaning, I slump against the rock. "Why did

you let up, Sadie? You were so *right* the entire time." Only raw emotion flows out in the words.

"I finally asked Mom what to do. She said sometimes when a man has something in his mind, you could go crazy trying to convince him otherwise. She said to let it go, be watchful, and let things play out."

I whimper at my stupidity! I'd been so taken by Mahloan from the first second I found her dangling off the cliff that I couldn't, no, I *wouldn't* see the truth. *Now the enemy has the compass!*

"Well, remind me to listen to you next time."

She grins. "Absolutely!"

"We better get to the visitor center, where I can get a location on the compass," Ethan says. "What if he gets on a plane?"

A low growl rumbles in my chest. Even if we get the compass back, I'm sure he'll have taken pictures of it!

"He doesn't know Cassidy was trying to create fakes. At least I was careful to keep that part from

Mahloan. The airplane though is a logical worry," Sadie says.

We lurch to our feet, legs tangling in the tight space. "Hurry! He already stole the cave artifacts. There's no telling what the man is capable of!"

We race across the desert back toward Delicate Arch. The sun pounds on my head, and I know the burning sensation of sun poisoning isn't far off. When we reach Mom and Dad, I dump a bottle of water over my head, and as the feeling recedes, I decide to tell how Hooknose followed us and took the compass. "Um, Mom, Dad...Mahloan was also working with Hooknose."

I knew they feel my pain. Every second on the hike to the truck and the drive to the visitor center feels like a lifetime. A hollow feeling rests in my pocket where the compass should be. My heart pounds out only one rhythm: *get it back. Get it back. Get it back. What if we don't?*

-25-

"I've got a signal!" Ethan is standing on the truck roof at the visitor center parking lot, holding his phone high.

"You'll never guess where he's hiding."

"The AIRPORT?" I shout, hands on my cheeks in horror.

"Nope. Devils Garden Campground!" he says.

I collapse to the sizzling asphalt. "Ouch!"

I sigh, *How stupid can I be to let Hooknose get my compass?* I sure hope I never see Mahloan again. I'm not sure what I would do.

"Let's go!" Sadie jumps into the truck.

"Mom's still inside. She had to use the restroom,"

Dad says, leaning against the hood. With a collective groan, we pile into the truck, waiting for her.

"Look, we can see the exact path he took with the compass." Ethan points to his screen where a little white line winds around the park.

"When did you put the air tag on there?" I ask, noting the length of the trail.

"Two nights ago while you were sleeping. I dreamed about it, so I got up and put it in the middle of the night."

"Nice job," I mutter, feeling even lower. *I'd been the one to include Mahloan for every step of our search and therefore Hooknose too!*

"I should've known the second they both appeared at the Cove of Caves!" The words burst out.

Sadie smiles at me sadly, patting my arm. "At least we know the truth now, and we will get the compass back. Then we'll figure out what that weird teardrop thing is."

I blink rapidly, ready to blow a fuse.

"One thing at a time," Ethan encourages.

I don't think I can handle anything more than finding the compass right now.

Mom grins as she gets in. "I grabbed your Junior Ranger booklets! This will be your tenth badge to earn!"

I run my hand over my trusty pack. Nine bright ranger badges give the plain black fabric so much life and color. Thoughts of all our adventures bring a peaceful calm to my crazy emotions. We've been in some extremely tight spots before, and we're still together.

"At least they didn't get the real Navigem," I mutter, trying hard to find a bright side.

"That's the spirit, Isaiah! What's even better is they *think* they did!" Sadie turns to Dad in the driver's seat and cries out, "Onward!"

The closer we come to Devils Garden, the harder my fists tighten, all my energy focusing on one thing: having the compass back in my hands.

The sun is sliding downward, and we still do not know if Hooknose has moved since we lost reception about two feet from the visitor center, but there's only one road, and I've been scanning each car carefully. I'm fairly certain he's still in the campground as we pull in.

Ethan grins. "Game on!"

-26-

"Site 011." I shake my head as we home in on the last known position of the air tag. "He's been right here the entire time."

Sadie shivers. "That gives me the creeps too."

"Shh." Ethan steps off the road in the deep dusk, and we slink between two other campsites. Now we can see 011 from the rear.

The black SUV sits next to a very impressive tent. Actually, it looks more like a building with rooms and all.

We crouch in the dark as Hooknose steps from the tent. He's got a phone pressed to his ear, and he's speaking a strange language. I don't need to know the words to understand the tone. *He's extremely angry.*

"How does he get reception out here?" Sadie whispers.

"Satellite phone. Shh." Ethan never takes his eyes off old Hooknose.

I have to admit, lately Ethan's proved his worth, especially on what he calls "covert ops." If he hadn't planted that air tag… I shudder, studying the man before us.

He looks fit, like he'd definitely come out on top in a fight. He smashes a button on the phone and exhales a sharp breath. He leans on the hood of the SUV and then pulls the compass from his pocket!

Every muscle tenses as I long to rush him. Sadie lays a hand on my arm. "We need a distraction."

I hear a familiar sound and a rush of wings. "Chip!" Sadie whispers. "This might work."

Sighing, Hooknose pulls the fake Navigem from his other pocket and fingers its surface. Chip makes a happy purr as the moonlight catches in the blue glass. Sadie bites her lip, desperate not to distract the raven. He gives one joyful hop, studying Hooknose with one eye, then the other. His midnight wings spread, and Sadie pumps one fist as Chip swoops like a shadow out of the sky. Hooknose gives a startled shout, his hands raising to protect his face. Chip pulls up sharply. I see the fake gem glinting in his claws!

"NO! Bird, stop!" Hooknose's shout only forces Chip higher into the night. The man slams the compass onto the truck hood, sprinting after Chip.

I've almost launched for the compass when a second man steps from the tent complex.

"Distraction number two." Ethan grins, then rushes toward the back side of the tent. He leaps, his lanky arms and legs spread wide as he collides with the fabric. The huge tent balloons at the sudden air pressure and then starts collapsing.

"Hey!" the man shouts, turning toward the toppling tent complex.

Before I can even think, I'm sprinting for the

compass. Everything else blurs in my intense focus. I swipe it off the truck hood in one smooth motion, stifling a victorious cry. I veer around the truck, gripping the compass with two hands. Heavy footsteps pound, but they're not mine!

I twist a quick look over my shoulder. I*t's Hooknose!* With a growl, I force more speed. I can tell he's gaining on me!

"Psst!"

I'd know that hiss in a pit of snakes! I search for Sadie in the pale moonlight. She's running parallel to me a few yards away!

With a grimace, I pitch the compass to her. Hooknose swipes at it in midair but misses!

Sadie catches it, skids to a stop, and reverses directions. Her dark shirt makes her blend into the desert.

She's passed the tent now, but Hooknose is on her heels! I cut past the rear of site 011, where the fancy tent is now just a pile of fabric.

"Get her!" Hooknose shouts to his partner.

I leap a boulder, counting on Sadie's taking the right-hand path. She's fast, but Hooknose isn't giving up and the distance closes between them.

"AH!" Hooknose shouts, gripping his head. Chip has two claws full of his hair, and he's flapping hard as if he's planning on carrying the man away. The other man passes Hooknose as he struggles wildly, unable to grasp the flapping bird.

Sadie and the man race on the narrow trail. *She's got to tire out soon!* But a shadow emerges from the gloom. At first, I'm sure it's a lion, but no! It's Ethan poised as if he's diving into a pool! His trajectory intersects with the man's pumping legs, and they go down in a tangle!

Sadie jets away, the darkness swallowing her slim form. I make sure Ethan scrambles away safely; then we veer left, taking another way back to camp. Chip still seems determined to yank out every hair on Hooknose's head!

-27-

I skid into our tent, my chest pumping. “Do you have it?”

“Of course!” Grinning, Sadie hands me the compass, and I clutch it against my chest.

Ethan arrives, holding his side. “Is everybody all right?”

“The question is, are you?”

“Yeah.” He pants. “Just got a cramp where that guy’s knee caught me.”

I clasp his shoulder. “Ethan, you really made that happen! Nice moves!”

He grins. “Thanks, but what do you call a spy who bleaches his hair?”

I humor him since he did just outsmart two grown men, and ask, "What?"

"James *Blond!*"

"That is funny," I say, feeling generous with the compass heavy in my palm.

"Do you think Hooknose will try to get it back?" Sadie asks.

"Yes, but I don't think he'll do it tonight. He's been very careful not to reveal himself, and the last thing he wants is to be banned from the park like Uncle Elliot. So, I think we'll be safe here at camp where we would have lots of witnesses."

I hear a distinctly birdlike trill at the door. "Our hero has arrived!"

We find Chip hopping around with the fake Navigem clutched in one foot.

"Chip! What a good bird!" Sadie croons, petting his glossy head.

Chip carefully places a beak full of dark hair at her feet, nudging it toward her. "What is this?"

I laugh. "He attacked Hooknose, or the man

would've had you!" Ethan grins at the bird who has all his feathers fluffed up as though he's very important.

"You're so brave!" Chip climbs into her arms as she cuddles him.

"You know, he's extremely intelligent. He snatched that Navigem, then stashed it somewhere safe because he sure didn't have it when he was turning Hooknose's hair into lawn clippings. He must've gone back for it afterward," I say.

Ethan reaches for the fake, but Chip caws loudly glaring at him. "Okay, I see how it is. It's a gift for Sadie. Sure."

"What? You want to keep your hair?" I tease.

"Sure do! Can you imagine what an entire flock of ravens could do to a person?"

"A flock of crows is called a *murder,* and a flock of ravens is called an *unkindness!*" Sadie says as Chip scoops up the Navigem and places it gently in her hand. "I'm glad there's only one of you!"

Later, while lying on top of my sleeping bag

in the heat, Mahloan's betrayal consumes my thoughts. I'd been so completely blind—the exact opposite of what Uncle Elliot needed me to be.

As the hours pass, the anger cools, and I study what she'd done so carefully. *Does she even have a grandmother? Was she even in any danger when we first met?*

The crunch of tires on sand makes me freeze with the compass against my chest. Ethan twitches in his sleep. "No tomatoes. NO TOMATOES!" Then he rolls over.

Easing the zipper up, I peer out. The white SUV is stained in the bright purple and pink sunrise! I scramble out, sweat beading on my shoulder blades.

"Hello again!" the deliveryman says.

Soon, he's got my signature, which is looking the same each time now, and picture, and I'm alone with the slimmest envelope yet.

Retreating to the safety of the tent, I rip open the cardboard, barely remembering to breathe. I pull out only three sheets of modern paper. Each one is a copy of a letter written by the Sundance Kid to Etta Place, the woman he loved and apparently lost.

My beloved Etta,

The unthinkable has happened. I've shot Butch Cassidy. I need you here to sort things out. What's that? No, he's not dead. Not yet anyway. He's pulled through many a bullet wound before. Remember when we held up train number three?

Ah, how I miss you. Why did you have to go where I couldn't follow? Tell me, what should I do about Cassidy? He told me I was too stupid to use the compass or the blue orb. I'm tired of being his second. I'm a dangerous man in my own right. I proved that yesterday. Being Cassidy's sidekick is more like being his pack mule. I'm smarter than him, anyway.

Problem is, I know he hid them both a month ago near our second Hole-in-the-Wall.

I nearly shout in victory! We were right on that account. I clamp a hand over my mouth and keep reading.

But I've got to find those two items; then the treasure will be mine—ours.

The blue orb consumes my thoughts, just as you do, Etta. Last night I dreamed I found the orb, and you were standing there too. I sure hope it happens.

The letter smarts: Cassidy had been betrayed. I know exactly how that feels—how it burns deep inside. I clench my eyes to force down the feelings and pull out the next page, which is shorter by far.

Etta,

Butch got me back. Shot me in the leg. Maybe I'm not smarter than he is after all. He's hurt bad too, though I've never seen him so pale. Guess he didn't like me snooping around with that "flyer" and asking questions. That tells me I'm on the right trail.

I might see you sooner than I thought, Etta. This leg hurts like fire.

Sundance

Flyer? The word sticks in my brain as I pull out the last note.

Etta!

Turns out he left me notes, the way he used to! Strings of clues. That was before we parted ways. All I need to do is figure out the last one. My leg? It's getting better, some. I poured whiskey on it just like you'd have done. Oh, I wish you'd been here to do it. I need your smarts,

Etta, I need you.

Stepping out of the tent, I gaze at the slowly lighting sky, my thoughts swirling.

"Me too, Sundance," I say, longing for answers to that same code. Time isn't on my side either. The surging emotions surrounding Mahloan and the Navigem don't help me think clearly. Knowing that the Sundance Kid and Cassidy broke faith with each other stings like peroxide in a wound. Since my heart is already ripped up, it burns pretty bad.

The sunrise spreads its brilliant colors farther across the sky. Something Mom said to me at Glacier circles in my mind. *"Forgiveness is actually far more important for you than the other person. Bitter feelings of hurt don't poison anyone but you."*

The problem is I can't forgive Mahloan—not after what she did.

-28-

Everyone's up by now, and I pull myself out of a deep melancholy to tell them about the delivery. Sadie and Ethan pore over the letters as Mom hands me a bowl of oatmeal. "You okay, son?"

I shrug, unable to speak. It doesn't matter though; she already knows. Sighing, she sits next to me, hugging me with one arm as she strikes right to the point. "Nobody ever *feels* like forgiving someone. It's always a decision at first. You *decide* to change how you think about someone and the things they did; then it grows into true forgiveness. That's part of the reason we can't live according to our emotions or how we feel. Feelings are like a roller coaster, and they aren't very trustworthy. We have to do what's right whether or not we feel like it."

I sigh, leaning into her and nodding.

"I'VE GOT IT!" Ethan leaps up, dumping his oatmeal.

"Well, that spill is going to attract ants," Mom says.

"What is it?" Sadie asks, shielding the letters from the dripping oatmeal.

"I saw a billboard for it in Moab! The *"flyer"* is the key!" He's stonewalling, enjoying knowing something we don't.

"Spill it, Ethan," I say.

"He already did!" Sadie giggles.

"The Wright brothers had the first successful airplane flight in 1903. But that was all the way in North Carolina. Out here in the desert, a far more simplistic form of flight was more common." He pauses, and I groan. "Okay! A hot-air balloon! It's the center picture of the code!"

Eyes wide, I nod in agreement. "You're right!"

"We've got to float over the park with the compass in order to find the Navigem!"

I rush to the tent. "Dad! Can we take a hot-air balloon ride?"

His groggy voice is muffled. "Five more minutes."

I slip into the tent, shaking his shoulder. "Dad, we need to take a hot-air balloon ride!"

"Okay!" He clears his throat, his eyes still closed. "Okay."

"Can we go today?"

"Today?" he says in a groggy voice. "Yes, it's today."

"YES!" I leap up, smashing my head against the top of the tent. The entire thing wobbles.

"Wait. What did I just agree to?" He sits up, blinking rapidly.

"Thanks, Dad!"

Sadie, Ethan, and I don't let up until they drive to the visitor center so Mom can search for a hot-air balloon company.

"Here's one based only 30 miles from here," she mutters, scrolling on her phone. She puts it to her ear. "Hello, we would like a hot-air balloon ride for three kids." She pauses, and we all hold our breath. "You're booked for a *year?*"

We all groan, flopping back onto the truck seat. She hangs up then searches some more. "Sorry guys, that was the only balloon company in the area."

I hold my head in my hands, searching for another way. Mom's phone rings.

"Yes, I did."

My head pops up, ears straining to hear her next words. "You do? Perfect! Yes, we'll be there at two o'clock."

"What's at two?" Sadie is about to burst.

"The receptionist didn't know they had a cancellation today, but you'll be in a hot-air balloon at two o'clock!"

Our shouts make Mom and Dad cover their ears. The hours drag past, feeling more like a month.

"You've got the compass?" Sadie asks as we get in the truck.

"Yep. Safe and sound." I pat my bulging pocket.

"Can I see it?"

It takes a lot of effort to pull it out. "Here."

She's sitting between Ethan and me as she opens the levels. I watch the red desert go by, biting the inside of my lip as thoughts about Mahloan swirl. Determined, I choose forgiveness. *Mom was right, even though I have chosen to forgive, I don't feel like it.*

Sadie gasps, drawing my attention. "Look at this!"

I peer at the spot near the hinge on the second level. *There's a tiny hole, probably for a screw.*

"I need a paperclip!" she breathes.

Ethan pats his pockets. "Um, I got nothing. How about asking the walking hardware store?"

"Of course, I've got one. You never know when you might need it," I say, sifting through my pocket. There's a fire starter, a stick of gum, and an alcohol cleaning pad. I grin as I hand her a paperclip.

She unfolds the thin metal and inserts it into the hole.

"Careful!" I warn.

"I remember in the schematic there was a spring near the hinge that wasn't a part of it!" She presses in the paperclip, but nothing happens. "Aw!"

Dejected, she slumps, staring at the compass. I pull out the sheaf of papers, locating the schematic for that layer.

"It's on this page." She points to one, and I pull it out. Sure enough, it's for the second level, and I see the unusual set of springs and pads tucked near the hinge.

"Push it again; it might be stiff from being unused for so long."

She does, but there's still no response.

"Hang on," Ethan says. "This part of the compass hasn't been used for years. I bet it needs a little oil."

Heart pounding, I dig in my pack, knowing I have a canister of WD-40 somewhere. I like to oil my tools every so often; and after they rusted from the salt water in Acadia, I've kept some handy.

"Here!" I hold up the small blue can. Keeping the nozzle over the hole, I depress the red button. The truck fills with the distinct scent of the oil. "Water displacement 40. I guess the other 39 formulas didn't work."

Maybe we are like those scientists; maybe our fortieth attempt will finally succeed.

Sadie forces the paperclip in again, and the compass gives a shrill squeak. "That's a good sign! Let me douse it again."

This time, the paperclip slides in and keeps going. I hear what sounds like a muted sigh inside the compass as the side of level two releases and slides open!

"No way!" Our mouths drop open as we lean in to look.

-29-

A small drawer is lined with a deep blue velvet inset, with divots and strange metal nuggets! Fingers trembling, I pull one loose and hold it up. We stare at the strange piece, but I'm unable to come up with even one idea of what to do with it. Ethan takes one and drops it.

"Rats!" He contorts in the small space of the back seat until he finds it.

"Maybe we'd better keep them in their individual places."

Sadie takes Ethan's piece and snaps it back into the compass.

"Here's what we do know. Each piece is a slightly different size. Each one has a flat bottom. And almost all of them have rounded tops," I say.

"If you can draw some sort of meaning from that description, I'd be happy to hear about it," Ethan remarks with his nose smashed against the window. "No way!"

We're driving down a parched sandy road and a hot-air balloon is straight ahead! The brilliant red fabric has stripes of color around it, and it is so tall! *I didn't think a balloon ride would be this amazing!*

"It's got to be 50 feet high!" Ethan exclaims.

"More like 80! It's incredible!" Dad says, pulling up near the basket.

"Welcome to Desert Balloons! Are these our riders for today?" a slim young man asks. I notice that his brown eyes look happy.

"Yes, these three," Mom says, snapping pictures.

"Great, I'm Michael, your pilot today!"

"Pilot?" Ethan asks. "Do you have a license?"

"Sure do! I'm fully certified to give you kids the best views of Utah ever!"

I release a nervous chuckle, suddenly unsure. "Do you think we can see Arches National Park?"

Michael checks his phone. "Winds are at 10 mph to the southeast. Hot-air balloons mostly follow the wind although we can tack some by using thermal currents. Today it looks like that wind will take us directly over the park!"

"YES!" As we high-five each other, relief floods through me.

"We should get about two hours of flying time, so we'll be looking at a pickup area on the far side of the Colorado River. Our flight crews carefully track our route if your parents would like to stick with them!"

"That sounds great!" Mom kisses each of our foreheads. "Use your smarts and obey all the rules."

"Yes, Mom."

"Okay!" Michael claps his hands. "Climb aboard!"

Ethan goes first, clambering over the railing of the thick wicker basket. Soon we're all in, and my heart pounds at the thought of hanging from a gigantic piece of fabric.

"Here are the rules: don't lean over the railing."

"That's it?" Ethan says.

"Yep, as long as you stay in the basket, you'll be fine."

"Nice! How old do you have to be to become a pilot?"

"Fourteen years old for hot-air balloons." Michael grins at us.

"Don't get any ideas, Ethan!" I threaten, imagining Ethan taking control of such a huge aircraft.

I stare up at the massive balloon. It's open at the bottom end, and I can see all the way to the top. A ball of flames belches into the neck of the balloon, and I throw my hands over my head.

"It's all right." Michael releases a lever, and the flame stops. "We burn propane to keep the hood full and to achieve liftoff!" He leans over the rail and shouts, "Ropes away!"

The basket creaks, and I grip its edge as I feel it

leave the ground. Sadie squeals, waving at Mom and Dad who are getting smaller by the second!

"And we are in flight! Welcome to the air, kids!"

I gasp as I look out. *I can see for miles!* Entwined with the wonder of the ride is the stress that we'll miss whatever we're supposed to find.

Soon, we are so high that the roads look like threads and the rare patches of green farmland seem like stickers.

"Can we get lower over the park?" I ask.

"That shouldn't be a problem; we can control our altitude with ease. The hotter the air inside the balloon, the higher we go; the cooler it is, the lower."

"*Altitude* means *height,* right?" Sadie asks.

"You got it. The winds are cooperating, taking us toward the park now." Michael points ahead.

I gaze over the desert spreading before us, knowing a small blue gem is waiting for us to discover it. A sudden hot wind wafts over us, and the balloon veers away from the park.

-30-

"Not to worry!" Michael fires the burner long and loud. I'll get this straightened out."

"Don't we have to follow the wind?" Ethan cries.

"Exactly! We just need the *right* wind." As the balloon rises, Michael holds a bottle of shaving cream over the side, and let's out a long stream of white fluff. We watch it fall, wavering; then it floats away from Arches.

"We need to go higher!" Michael shouts.

Soon, he releases another jet of shaving cream. This time, it spreads out toward the park.

"Bingo!" He holds our altitude, and we now drift toward Arches.

"Perfect!" Sadie shouts as the balloon cools, and we descend closer to the magnificent Arches.

I can't tell if it's the height or pure worry, but my stomach feels less than happy.

"What if we miss it?" My knuckles are white on the wicker basket.

"Miss what?" Michael asks.

"I wish I knew!" I say over my shoulder.

"This is like looking at a map of the park!" Ethan says.

My breath catches in my throat. *A map?* Everything seems to freeze. *A map! Of course!* I yank wildly at the compass jammed as usual in my pocket. Fearing that I'll fumble it over the edge of the basket, I kneel, frantically inserting the paperclip.

"Sadie! What's the first arch you see?"

"Uh… I don't know its name!" she squeaks.

The tray finally pops out, and the squiggles on the face of level two take on a whole new meaning. *A map!* "No, I mean, what direction does it face?"

She grimaces. "North! South! I don't know!"

I stand, carefully keeping the compass lower than the basket.

"There," I align the first level compass with due north, then I take a piece from the tray and set it on the face of level two. It slides across the slick surface, and I nearly drop it. *That's not going to work. The piece keeps shifting around.*

"Wait!" We're now floating directly over the first arch, and Ethan strains to look under the basket. "Try this piece!"

He taps one toward the back of the blue velvet inset. I put the first one away, then set his piece on the face. It zings out of my fingers and across the surface! It twists to a stop near one side of the compass!

We all gasp, watching as the first squiggle slowly twists, lining up with the piece now locked into place! Then, a second later, a letter surfaces near the top of the first piece, "it's an M!"

"No way," Ethan whispers.

"Yes way," Sadie whispers back.

"What's the next arch?" I demand, running my fingers over the remaining pieces.

"It's a small one, real thin!" Sadie says, pointing ahead.

Biting my lip, I select the thinnest piece of metal and set it near the opposite end of the squiggle that had moved. "Yes!"

It snaps into place in the next squiggle and aligns itself! "This one revealed an O!"

"Hello, Chip!" Sadie calls, cupping her hands over her mouth and yelling loudly.

"Do you know that bird?" Michael asks, as Chip wheels closer.

"Sure do. Hey, pretty boy!" Chip soars next to the basket, tilting his tail to move closer.

"Wow! I've never seen flying from a bird's-eye view," Ethan says. Chip lands on the wicker basket cooing at Sadie.

"Well, that's a first!" Michael says.

"Arches!" I cry, absorbed by what the compass is revealing.

"Okay! This one is really long!" Ethan calls.

I select the longest piece and set it on the board.

"Perfect!" I wait for everything to finish moving. "Hey! So far we have MOA!"

"I see Delicate Arch!" Sadie shouts.

"Okay!" I search the remaining pieces for one that's narrow at the top and twisted. The magnets under the board seem to be stronger the more pieces I align, and it nearly sucks this one out of my grip before I place it on the board. "B! Moab, it spells Moab! Ha!"

I sag against the basket; it really *is* a map! "There are only two more pieces! What do you see?"

"What's that sound?" Ethan asks.

"I don't care what you hear. I need to know what you see!"

"It's a double arch!" Sadie says.

One of the remaining pieces has a dip on the top of it. I snap it onto the board; and though it reveals no more letters, now there's only one squiggle out of place.

"I think you should care about that sound!" Ethan's voice has a tinge of desperation.

Hurrying, I set the last piece on the board, and an X appears at the end of the line!

"YES!"

"NO!" Ethan cries, pointing. "That's a drone!"

The sound finally reaches me inside the basket. It's a steady mechanical whir getting louder every second. Still, I study level two, locking its map in my memory. I look up to see Michael frowning.

"Aviation laws prohibit flying a drone within 50 feet of a hot-air balloon!"

"Well, that doesn't seem to matter at the moment!" Ethan is focused on the large black drone now hovering only a foot or two from our basket!

"I have a sinking feeling that I know whose drone that is," Sadie whispers, her eyes wide.

"My plan is to avoid sinking until we're ready to land!" Michael swats at the drone with his hand, but it dodges expertly.

Chip's head is following its motion as his feathers fluff up. The drone rises above the basket, and I get my first full view of it. I shield the compass from the camera as it tilts toward me.

"Hooknose," I growl.

"Get out of here!" Sadie shouts, waving her hands at it. Chip lets out an ear-piercing crow, his movements growing sharper.

The noise increases as the drone shoots upward. Michael cries, fear tinting his voice.

"What's the worst that could happen?" Ethan shouts, leaning out to monitor the drone.

"If it tears our funnel, we go down!"

-31-

"What?" My voice cracks as I stand, keeping the compass low.

"No!" The veins in Michael's neck stand out as he too cranes his neck upward to watch. The drone backs off a few feet, hovering about halfway up the thinner part of our funnel.

"He wouldn't!" Sadie cries.

"He *would!*" I shout, completely helpless to stop Hooknose. The distance to the ground isn't such a beautiful picture anymore; it's a quick drop with a fast ending!

The drone tilts toward the balloon! Sadie screams, Chip caws, and Ethan roars.

In a flash, Chip launches after the drone, and the two black birds collide only inches from the thin fabric!

A puff of feathers floats all around us. I grip the basket as it tilts crazily.

"Chip?" Sadie whispers, covering her face. Then a black blob rockets past the basket.

"No!" Tears run down Sadie's face.

Ethan follows the plummeting object, watching closely. "Get it, Chip!" he cheers.

Sadie gasps, rushing forward to look. The raven is streaking straight toward the ground, the drone helpless in his claws! From here, it looks as if he's going to crash; but at the last second, he pulls up, letting the drone go. It smashes against the red rocks.

Chip swoops in again, snatching the largest piece that's left, his wings pumping as he flies back toward us. He reaches our level, his tail flaring as he flips in midair, throwing the chunk of drone with wires sticking out! The plastic falls; but he zooms in again, claws crunching hard.

He whirls toward us, landing on the rail, cawing over and over. What's left of the drone dangles under him.

"Good bird!" we all cry together.

-32-

"There seems to be a river in our way." Ethan's got his hands on his hips, sweat pouring down as we stare at the Colorado River. We'd overlaid the compass map with a map of Arches, aligning the starting point with Moab, and found the path led straight out of the park—*onto Mahloan's land.* I sigh, wishing I could remember where the boundaries of her property were and that the "X" was anywhere else.

"We knew that much," I say, pulling out the climbing harnesses I'd packed.

"Hang on," Dad says. "I agreed to hike off trail with you, but rappelling down to the river? Um… not so sure about that."

"Please, Dad? The X lands right about here somewhere. It could be on this side of the river or the other. We've got to at least check!" I sigh, harnesses dangling. I know the Navigem is most likely on the far side, but I'm unwilling to leave anything unexplored.

"Please!" We all beg together.

Dad walks to the edge of the steep drop-off looking down at the Colorado's blue waters far below. We'd followed Salt Wash all the way from Wolfe Ranch to here.

"The cliff isn't nearly as steep on this side, anyway," I say, as we all step into our harnesses. "We've rappelled loads of times, Dad."

If Mom had come, we would have zero chance of getting to go down. But Dad's another story altogether! *We might just succeed.*

"If you head down that way, you could probably get almost to the river," he says, studying the landscape.

We grin at each other; then Ethan's face goes

slack and turns white. Eyes wide, I turn. The hot-air balloon is floating this way!

"It can't be…" Sadie says, grimacing.

"Only one way to know." Ethan pulls binoculars from his pack. I clip our harnesses together with sturdy sections of rope as Ethan growls. "It's Hook-nose!"

Biting my lip, I scan the area. I spot a pile of boulders at the edge of the cliff that will hide us. "Come on!"

The balloon is low, skimming along and heading straight toward us on a swift wind. Tied together, we rush into the boulder field to hide. My stomach clenches. *Did Hooknose get a snapshot of the complete compass map after all? How could he possibly end up right here?*

My mouth goes dry as sharp anger rises. If I hadn't trusted Mahloan, Hooknose would've been five steps behind! I punch my thigh as I kneel next to Ethan and Sadie. A huge shadow blankets us, and I hold my breath as the balloon itself hovers directly above. It's so close the wicker basket's familiar creaking is clear.

Ethan cocks his head, gripping the carabiner that's clipped to his harness by a short length of rope. We stare hard at the basket as it passes over.

My heart burns, knowing the enemy will be across the Colorado in a few seconds: far closer to the Navigem than we are. As the basket passes over, Ethan leaps high, snapping the carabiner onto one of the holding straps on the basket.

I think my heart turned to stone for a second. "Ethan!"

The entire world just changed.

"We can stop him!" Ethan whispers, pulling back on the rope. He skids, but the hot-air balloon doesn't even notice as the desert wind forces it past the cliff!

"Ethan!" I squeak as the ropes between him and Sadie pull tight, and she stumbles forward.

"No, no, no, no, no!"

I release a sharp breath and then I'm yanked forward like a train car behind a giant engine!

"We can stop it!" Ethan is still straining, his feet inching toward the edge! He gives an awkward yelp as he leaves the ground!

Sadie turns to me, terror on her face; then she's airborne too, dangling below the basket! I watch the taut rope draw me to the edge of the cliff. My breath comes in hard puffs as I grip the rope, straining backward.

My feet slide over the edge, and I swing out over nothing!

-33-

I scramble, fighting the wild motion that could tilt me upside down and right out of this harness. I grip the rope and try not to think how far down it is to the water. By twisting slowly, I see Dad come into view standing on the cliff's edge. He throws up his arms in bewilderment.

"Why?" His shouted word barely reaches me, and I dare not make a peep lest Hooknose find out we're here. *Who knows what he would do?*

I will myself to take a breath as the balloon slows over the river; then it jerks, making me flinch. I hear the burner fire, then Michael's voice. "We're in a bad downdraft over the river! The air must be colder here. Seems like we've gained 200 pounds!" He fires the burner again, and the balloon gains some altitude.

Ethan hisses above me. I look up; the far side of the river is much higher. Its cliffs rise in sharp faces.

"Come on!" I whisper as we cruise toward them on a collision course. The roar of the burner doesn't let up, but the balloon responds sluggishly with our extra weight.

The rope wiggles, making me spin. Sadie's freaking out, struggling in her harness.

"Sadie!" I whisper, desperate for her to be still. "Just close your eyes!"

She shut them tight, freezing.

"Come on!" Michael shouts, as things rain down around us. A few water bottles, then the heavy sandbags that were tied to the outsides of the basket. I watch them fall, but they drop for so long that it makes me dizzy.

We're almost against the cliffs! The balloon

shivers, catching the hot air from the approaching rocks! We lift suddenly. My mind races, hating the thought of dangling here if the balloon reaches a high altitude again. Frantically, I try to dig out my multi-tool from my back pocket, but it's jammed inside the harness!

I tilt forward, my fingers finally touching it. The motion starts me spinning again, and I grimace at the sight of the river and what will happen if I fall.

With a final yank, the tool comes free. "Sadie!"

She opens her eyes and squawks.

"Catch!" I throw the tool, not giving her any time to think. She swipes the spinning tool in mid-air and grips the rope again.

"Throw it up to Ethan!" I whisper.

She moans, the cliffs are only a few feet away. The basket will clear, but I'm not so sure about us! We're almost high enough. More sandbags plummet past us as the balloon surges upward again. If Ethan misses Sadie's throw, we could be in for a very long ride!

He catches it! I slump against my rope, then something touches my feet!

"Eh!" I open my eyes; scrubby bush is scraping my legs, and I tuck into a ball as I smash against the top of the cliff.

Sadie's feet are just above it as the balloon tugs us over the land. Twisting at the impact, I scrape the last few feet, then I'm on top of the cliff! Intense relief fills me, and I hiss at Ethan, "Cut the rope, NOW!"

I'm dragged along the burning rocks, and I can't get to my feet because of the tangle of ropes. Ethan's sawing like crazy on the rope above us.

"Hurry!" Sadie hisses.

With a snap, the rope lets loose, and I barely have a heartbeat to prepare for Sadie and Ethan's sudden arrival on top of me.

"Ouch." My face is smashed against the scorching desert as they scramble off me.

"We lived!" Sadie has her hands over her mouth.

Finally free of our weight, the balloon lurches.

As it floats past, Hooknose appears, looking out of the basket at us.

"Hey!" He points toward us still tangled in the ropes, his face reddening.

"Run!" I shout, and we stumble into the cover of some rocks.

Hooknose is bellowing, but the wind breaks up his words, and I glance out of our cover. My heart nearly hits my toes. He's thrown a rope over the side of the balloon, and he is clambering down!

-34-

As Hooknose's feet hit the ground, I lurch behind the rocks, my lungs pumping. The compass now feels way too heavy in my pocket. He knows it belongs to me; Mahloan had told him that much.

"Ethan, take the compass!" I slap it into his palm, a plan formulating. "We've got to split up! There's only one of him, and he wants the compass, so he'll follow me!"

Sadie is shaking her head.

"Mahloan's house should be that way a quarter of a mile or so. We'll meet within sight of it!"

Ethan tucks the compass into his pocket, nodding his understanding.

"Take good care of Sadie," I say, and before fear can make me fail, I rush out in full sight of Hooknose!

I run, veering toward a maze of boulders. Before I disappear inside, I twist. *He's coming!* His face is an angry shade of red that lends more speed to my legs.

I leap over an outcropping, trying to keep my bearings by the sun's position. My lungs heave, the dry desert heat presses in, and I twist around boulders. Careening around a corner, I slam into something soft and warm.

Forward motion forces my arms around the human shape, and information floods my brain in that crazy motion. *It's Mahloan!* Growling, everything in me recoils; but with Hooknose right behind, I dare not let her give me away again!

Giving into our tumble, I slap one hand over her mouth, grab her around the ribs, and gain my feet. Then I drag her behind an outcropping. Heart slamming, I watch Hooknose rush past. Mahloan's frantic breath rushes from her nose over my hand, but she doesn't struggle.

Seconds tick past, and I let her go. I back away, eyes smoldering. She turns to me in tears. I won't believe them; she's too good of an actress.

"Isaiah, I..."

"Don't say anything, Mahloan. Actions speak louder than words." I glare at her and then spin, leaving her behind. Cutting back toward our meeting place, I find myself trapped in a deep canyon. With a groan, I sprint back toward the exit. *If Hooknose finds me here...* I shut down those thoughts, longing for a drink. Getting air past my dry throat is hard.

A scream makes me skid to a stop; my hair stands on end. I listen hard. *Was that Sadie?* Energy sizzles across my chest, and I clench my fists as the scream reverberates again; I'm positive it's Mahloan's voice. *She won't trick me again that way!* Clenching my jaw, I turn in the other direction, needing space between us.

"Get away!" Mahloan's desperate tone does nothing to me. She's trying to draw me into another trap, and I won't… *Hold on.* Stopping to stand still, I hold my breath scanning for the sound.

My blood runs cold as a low growl rises into a high-pitched snarl. *Mountain lion.* I swallow hard, knowing the one who's been taking her sheep has lost its fear of humans. I bow my head at the war taking place inside.

With a moan, I run toward the sound. *If it's a trap, so be it. I'd never forgive myself if it wasn't.* Inside, it seems as if a giant weight is crushing me. I'd give just about anything not to have known Mahloan was out here. *But I can't turn back now.*

Another desperate scream draws me forward, and I climb the crumbling foot of a tower. Cresting its edge, I see Mahloan pressed against the red rock, tears streaming as she holds a branch between her and the lion.

The animal is much bigger than I had imagined. The mountain lion's thick tail sweeps sharply behind it. A growl makes my skin crawl as it lashes at her with its wide front paw. Before I can think, a blistering hot rock is in my hand. I whip it with all my might at the beast.

It whirls toward me, its gold-green eyes mesmerizing. Massive fangs make all the strength drain from my muscles. Mahloan sprints to the right, and everything becomes sheer chaos! The lion leaps onto her as I skid down the loose rocks on a collision course!

-35-

I slam into tan fur, bellowing as I kick at the brute's head. He backs off, and I pull Mahloan to her feet in a heartbeat. She sags against me, whimpering. *Her arm is bleeding!*

I spread my arms and legs, still shouting, but the lion still rushes us! I scoop up another rock, as I crouch in front of Mahloan.

The lion leaps, I swing. The rock connects with his jaw, turning aside his attack! The massive creature circles and then slinks away! I turn back to Mahloan, inspecting her arm. It's not as bad as I had thought. Actually, the injury looks more like a scrape from falling on the rocks.

"Why did you come back for me?" she whispers, her green eyes brimming with tears.

I sigh, trying to sort out my thoughts. "I decided to forgive you…but that doesn't mean I trust you." My voice comes out sharp, and she cowers.

"We better put some distance between us and the lion." I set off, expecting her to follow. I turn to look back. "Hurry."

As she staggers to her feet, memories of our meeting flood my mind. "Were you even in danger on that cliff? Do you even have a grandmother?" The questions spill out, and I wait for an answer.

"Yes, I would've fallen…" She swallows hard. "I was looking for you…to find the Navigem, but I fell." She hangs her head, and I frown, walking away.

"Wait, please!" She trots next to me. "Can't you understand? I didn't know you then; all I knew was there was suddenly a way to save the ranch and my Gran! But then you…you became my friend! And I…" She sobs, and I turn to look at her, folding my arms over my chest.

"I was torn up inside! How can I choose to let my Gran lose everything when she is so sick? But deceiving you killed me!"

I grunt, steeling my heart against her words. Trudging forward, I study the position of the sun. I had gotten turned around in the towers.

Mahloan grabs my arm. "Shh!"

Ahead, I hear the crunch of footsteps! Mahloan tugs me into a side canyon, and I have no time to wonder if she's being truthful. We sprint forward until Mahloan ducks under a low bridge of stone. We huddle in the tight, cool space, watching the path.

Hooknose strides before us, but all I can see are his legs. He stops, and I tense. *We're trapped here! Stupid! One peep from Mahloan, and I'm toast!*

-36-

I look at her, but she remains silent, watching Hooknose walk away, searching for me. Moments pass as we wait for the distance to increase.

"They came and took our sheep yesterday," Mahloan says so softly that I almost don't hear her voice. "What was left of them anyway. That's why the lion came after me; there's no more easy prey." She runs a finger around the wound on her arm.

I dig in my back pocket, pulling out an alcohol pad. As I cleanse the wound, she cringes.

"We've only got three more weeks before they take the ranch too." Her voice is as empty as her eyes. "I failed Gran...and you."

"You said Hooknose was going to pay it off."

"He lied."

The brokenness I hear in those two words is like a punch in my gut. Her green eyes find mine flashing with emotion. "I can't bear what I did, Isaiah—not after you saved me and became my friend."

Maybe I'm dumb, but I believe her. My heart hurts for everything that's ripping her life apart. I hold out my hand. "Come on, let's go." With that gentle tone, I offer a truce.

She looks at me in surprise.

"Mahloan, friends help each other, remember?"

She slips her hand into mine, and I pull her to her feet. "We're meeting Sadie and Ethan over near your place; then we will find the Navigem."

We both look up as a shadow flashes over us. Chip wheels sharply, cruising above us. Not finding Sadie, he flaps away again.

"How did you get across the river?" she asks.

I smile, thinking of Ethan's terrible plan.

-37-

"Aaaand, Isaiah, why am I not surprised that you show up with Mahloan?" Sadie says, crossing her arms.

Mahloan's shoulders slump at her harsh words. I cringe inside, recalling how cold I had been to her only moments ago.

I nudge Mahloan. She nods, then pours out her story. Sadie turns toward the starkly empty barnyard beside us with one gate hanging open; it's an obvious testament to Mahloan's story.

She sighs. Losing the animals hits her soft spot. "Okay. I am sorry for the way things worked out."

"Navigem?" Ethan says, his lips stained purple.

Ethan hands over the compass, and I reset the second level, my pulse spiking as I watch the pieces snap into place.

"Wow!" The wonder in Mahloan's voice fills me with awe too.

The letters in Moab slowly appear and then the X at the end.

"When did that turn red?" Sadie shrieks, pointing to the X.

I scowl at it, finding the center of the black X is now a bright red. "It couldn't…"

"Couldn't what?" Ethan asks, but I'm too wrapped up in thought to answer. I turn in a full circle, my mind racing.

"Couldn't WHAT?" Sadie insists.

"This compass belonged to Robert Perry, a famous explorer." I squint, traveling through history in my mind. "He's the one who designed this map and had this compass fabricated."

"So, the Navigem isn't here?" Ethan asks, his jaw dropping.

I shake my head, "Without a doubt, Cassidy must have stolen the compass at some point, and he must've figured out how to use the map on the second level. That means he had been to this place marked with an X. He knew it would be the safest place to hide the precious Navigem."

"Whew!" Ethan wipes his brow.

"This…" I suck in a huge breath. "This find could be way bigger than just the Navigem. Robert Perry wouldn't have designed and had such an intricate map created for nothing."

"The red X, Isaiah! I want to know why it's turning red!" Sadie stomps her foot.

I nod. "The hiding place must have a strong magnetic field—one that's causing the red metal to surface within the center as we get closer."

We all lean over the compass, take a bearing, and I grin. "Let's go!"

We rush toward Mahloan's small house, but the red fades. A shadow rises over us, and Chip caws, spotting Sadie.

"Let's head west!" Mahloan points back toward the red towers where we'd lost Hooknose.

"We must be extra careful in there. Between Hooknose and the lion, it's going to be dangerous."

"Wait!" Ethan exclaims. "Did you say *lion?*"

-38-

I creep forward, easing under a hot red cliff. The X is now completely red! Silently, I point at the compass. Everyone scowls, looking around. *There's nothing here but more desert!* Chip takes off from Sadie's shoulder, disappearing over the cliff top. A moment later, he's back with something green in his beak. He lands on Sadie's outstretched arm, and she takes the leaf.

Mahloan gasps and whispers, "Bathua! Where did he get it?" She breathes, studying the cliffs. Chip waddles happily up to Sadie's shoulder. He bounces there, his feathers fluffing up more by the minute. *He senses something.*

I scan the tangle of towers and boulder fields, jerking as a shadow moves to our right. My sudden grip on Sadie's arm alerts both Ethan and Mahloan.

Slowly, Ethan eases backward behind the tower. Setting each foot carefully, we follow him, holding our breath. I ease one eye back around the edge as my blood runs cold!

Hooknose is on our trail! I whip around, but Mahloan's face is deathly pale, and she's pointing behind Ethan.

"L…li…lion!" she breathes. At her words, Ethan's eyes go wide, slowly turning. The tawny lion is locked on Ethan, stalking closer. Frantic, I swipe the compass pieces off level two and the red X fades. I slide the compass closed and jam it into my pocket.

Chip takes flight. The lion inches closer, low to the ground, his muscles bunching.

"Ahem…" Ethan clears his throat. "Mr. Lion, nice to meet you. I'd like to inform you I am not a sheep, but…" The lion continues to slink forward.

"I do know some sheep jokes!" His voice cracks as high above, Chip folds his wings, now a black torpedo rocketing toward the cougar.

The lion growls as Chip smashes into his head. Chaos breaks out as we run, the animals fight, and Hooknose shouts from somewhere behind us!

Time turns into syrup as strangely as the red X that consumes me. *We've got to be standing right on Robert Perry's treasure!* I blink. Everything is crazed motion behind, but all I can see is the sprig of Bathua and that red X.

Ethan's bellowing…well…screaming, but I'm locked in, staring at the wall of sandstone before me. I run my hand over it as someone slams into my back. Undisturbed, I study the rock carefully. *This small section looks different somehow, rougher than the rest.*

"Eeeeeehh!" Sadie, Ethan, and Mahloan plow into my back, and since my arm is already extended, I become a boy-sized battering ram. I gasp as my fist goes straight through the odd patch of stone! I shut my eyes as my face hits next, and time snaps back to its frantic pace!

The lion is snarling, Chip's black wings beat above us, and I fall forward...***and continue to fall!***

-39-

I flail in the air, plummeting downward. I can sense the others above me and barely catch a breath before plunging into deep water! It bubbles around me, shockingly cold in the desert heat.

We pop up like gophers, treading the crystal water and sucking in air.

“Watch out!” I cry, as a massive tumble of rocks comes down from the place we broke through the stone wall! The rocks hit the water like mini-explosions, and we swim as fast as possible for a low shelf of rock.

“Wait…” I say, and we all freeze perfectly still, gripping the ledge.

A shrill outcry echoes above. *Hooknose!* The lion's chilling snarl grows; then the punishing report of a gun makes us all recoil. A moment passes, and we hear another gunshot farther down the valley!

"He didn't see us!" Ethan grins, his hair plastered to his forehead.

"Hooknose only found one angry lion!" We laugh, pulling ourselves up onto the ledge.

"What is this place?" Sadie reaches for a bunch of bright green vines curling down the rocks. "It's like a hidden garden!"

Mahloan rushes forward crying, "Bathua! Look! It's everywhere!"

We're in a tight circular canyon with no exit save the small hole where I had broken through. I rub my raw knuckles, grinning. *This paradise we've discovered in the middle of the desert is Robert Perry's hiding place!*

Tears flow down Mahloan's cheeks as she runs her hands through the plentiful bathua. I turn, scanning the small area and bite my lip. I see no obvious hiding place for the Navigem. Soon we've explored every crevice of the hidden garden.

"Nothing," I say, sitting heavily on the ledge with my legs dangling in the pool. *I'm still a failure.* "No Navigem."

Mahloan's soft hand finds my shoulder. "Don't give up yet. Think about it. Why isn't this water stagnant? I mean, it should be full of algae, right?"

I shrug, feeling empty inside.

"Ethan, do you have some of that electrolyte powder?" she asks.

"Sure thing." He pulls out a slim plastic package from his back pocket and hands it to her.

She pours the purple powder into the pool. We watch the bright colors swirl around and then it rushes under the ledge!

"Wait, do you think…" I say, watching the current. "That's got to lead to another pool!"

I dive in, the water a shock on my skin. I float, feeling for the current.

"It's not strong; I'm going!" Gulping a breath, I

dive as Mahloan and Sadie shout my name, but I'm already stroking into the darkness under the ledge. I see a glimmer of blurry light ahead!

All in, I pull hard toward the light. I burst into the light, treading water in a circle. *I'm now in a dome-shaped cave!* Only one tiny hole high above lets in the filtered light. I'm longing to explore, but I know on the other side Sadie is losing her composure as she worries about me. Knowing I can reach air, I make the swim back with ease.

I sputter to the surface. They're all in the water, their faces worried. "It's a cave! Hurry!"

We dive, popping up in a place hidden for 100 years. With water streaming down her face, Sadie gasps and points. "Look!"

One wall of the cave is covered in lines of writing. I can't read the language, but at its center is a circular map! It's full of strange symbols and markings.

And there on a rock ledge sits the Navigem! Reverently, I pick it up, surprised by its weight. The etched Navigem is beautifully polished, and it's a deeper blue than the fakes.

Sadie selects a strange metal disc full of holes from the shelf.

"*Whaaahoooo!*" Ethan shouts, leaping back into the pool in a cannonball. I grip the Navigem, relief flooding my mind.

Mahloan grins at me, and I must admit I'm so glad to have her here. "You know, Mahloan, technically, this gem belongs to you."

Sadie's face goes white, and Ethan suddenly stops splashing.

She nods. "It is on my land." She looks carefully at each of us. "But the Navigem is yours."

She can't hide the tears that glimmer in her eyes, knowing this won't be her land for very long.

"Hey!" Ethan says, tasting the water, nibbling it like a rabbit.

"Ethan, must you always taste everything?" Sadie asks. But Ethan ignores her, swimming to the far wall, climbs out, and then licks the wall.

"I didn't mean *everything*!" Sadie screeches.

"It's salty."

"Oh, joy," Sadie says in a flat tone.

"No, I mean it *is salt.*"

With a start, I scan the far wall. The entire surface is uniform, a reddish tint mixed in with the white color.

"That's a pretty big deposit of salt," I say.

"Isn't Utah known for its salt mines?" Ethan asks.

"Yes," Mahloan says.

"Developing a salt mine is an extremely *lucrative* business," Ethan insists.

Mahloan's eyes widen. "Is it possible that Gran owns a salt mine?"

"It is a lot of salt," I say, grinning at her. "Besides, I feel sure my Uncle Elliot would be happy to assist you and your grandmother in any way possible to help you keep this place in exchange for your permission to study the map and markings in this cave. That will give you time to start your salt mine." *With our finding the Navigem and the hidden secret in the compass, I feel quite sure Uncle Elliot will involve us in his findings. I can't wait!*

Her hands fly to her face, her green eyes happier than I've ever seen them.

The light flickers out, and we all look up. Chip has his head jammed into the small hole, purring at Sadie. The raven reminds me of the outside world. I suddenly imagine Dad's rushing back to Mom and saying, "Honey? I lost the kids."

Grinning at the thought, I know we're going to hear it for Ethan's antics at the river. I look back at Mahloan.

"Finding the Navigem with a *friend* made this time in the Arches perfect."

To find out what the Navigem reveals,
watch for the next adventures
of the **Campground Kids**.